Ivy couldn't breathe.

She didn't know where to look. It was bad enough that she'd seen *all* of Giaco today. Now she was supposed to...date him? Pretend to fall in love with him? She was not an actress. How would any of this work?

She found herself drawn to look at Giaco again, telling herself it was the horror of this that was making her seek him out for some kind of confirmation that he was hearing the same things she was.

But all she saw was that too-dark jade, so mocking, and currently filled with what looked like some kind of glee.

"I'm sure that sweet, virtuous, stepsister Ivy and I can work it out," Giaco said, though that gaze of his was fastened to Ivy, and there was nothing about it that suggested he saw her as *sweet* or virtuous in any way. "As long as you're aware, my soon-to-be beloved and bride, that I require a not inconsiderable amount of fucking. Daily. Can you handle that?"

TO HAVE & TO HATE

CAITLIN CREWS

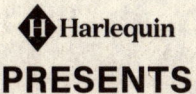

Harlequin
PRESENTS

MIX
Paper | Supporting responsible forestry
FSC® C021394

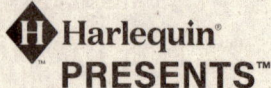

Recycling programs for this product may not exist in your area.

ISBN-13: 978-1-335-21376-1

To Have & To Hate

Harlequin Enterprises ULC
22 Adelaide St. West, 41st Floor
Toronto, Ontario M5H 4E3, Canada
www.Harlequin.com

HarperCollins Publishers
Macken House, 39/40 Mayor Street Upper,
Dublin 1, D01 C9W8, Ireland
www.HarperCollins.com

Printed in Lithuania

USA TODAY bestselling, RITA® Award–nominated and critically acclaimed author **Caitlin Crews** has written more than one hundred and thirty books and counting. She has a master's and PhD in English literature, thinks everyone should read more category romance and is always available to discuss her beloved alpha heroes— just ask. She lives in the Pacific Northwest with her comic book–artist husband, is always planning her next trip and will never, ever read all the books in her to-be-read pile. Thank goodness.

Books by Caitlin Crews

Harlequin Presents

Forbidden Royal Vows
Greek's Christmas Heir
Her Accidental Spanish Heir
Forbidden Greek Mistress
An Heir for Christmas
Sicilian Devil's Prisoner
King's Heir of Hate

Notorious Mediterranean Marriages

Greek's Enemy Bride
Carrying a Sicilian Secret

Work Wives to Billionaires' Wives

Kidnapped for His Revenge

Visit the Author Profile page
at Harlequin.com for more titles.

CHAPTER ONE

Ivy Amis had once declared—after having to put up with entirely too many self-congratulatory speeches from those who should have chosen respectful silence on the occasion of her mother's funeral—that returning to her former stepfather's ostentatious Italian castle would occur only if she first crawled the length of England on hands and knees. Over broken glass. Twice.

In fairness, that was how it felt now that she was actually doing it five years later.

Even the ancient rolling hills of Tuscany, with so many cypress trees dressed in pockets of mist in formation along the edges of old, lush vineyards, failed to mask the sensation of too many sharp edges pressing into her flesh.

Her typical reaction to anything having to do with the Tavian family.

Made worse now that she was actually back in their vicinity.

It had taken exactly one phone call to be thrown back into the worst memories of her teenage years. Umberto's oily, patronizing voice. That knowing chuckle, as if he'd expected this call all along—which he probably had. As if all the work she'd done to turn her back on this place and these people had been nothing but an exercise in futility.

A silly girl's attempt to escape reality.

She'd nearly told him where he could go right then. It had hurt her jaw to keep it clenched so tight.

But she told herself to shake it off and shape up, sitting there in the back seat of one of Umberto's fleet of shiny, obnoxious Range Rovers. He had insisted that he send his plane to come pick her up. That she not lift a single finger to get herself to Tuscany—something that a person who didn't know Umberto might consider a kindness.

Ivy, sadly, knew her former stepfather—the man who had made her lovely mother so desperately miserable— entirely too well.

There wasn't a single thing the creepy old man did that wasn't about control.

Especially the things he dressed up in solicitous disguises.

She looked out the window and reminded herself that she was no longer the awkward girl she'd been when she'd first been dragged here against her will, forced to leave her home behind to follow this whim of her mother's. On the contrary. These days Ivy was what this place had made her. There was a strength in that.

Besides, she was here for a purpose.

This wasn't her starry-eyed mother making up fairy tales in her head. This wasn't the notably romantic screen legend Alana Amis allowing a powerful and mysterious Italian to sweep her off her feet—and then sweeping up her daughter along with her because Alana had been lovely in so many ways but had never been one for boundaries.

Ivy smiled, remembering what her mother had said on that topic. *Darling, I am an* actor. *My life is about expanding* past *boundaries, not collapsing into them.* Something Alana had taken seriously.

This time Ivy had decided to come here of her own volition. This time, Ivy had decided that she would play Umberto's game and beat him.

Assuming that was possible given Umberto had been running his power plays since long before Ivy was born.

The Range Rover purred its way up the drive and then stopped at the imposing front door of the ancient castle that was habitually featured in architectural magazines. The sort of publications that liked to fawn over each and every one of Umberto's choices and suggesting his *discernment* in financial matters made him *keenly situated* in the *lexicon* of style. As if a corporate titan like Umberto—who had never polluted his business bona fides with an actual day of leisure in all the time Ivy had been forced to live with him—actually sat about poring over the incidental details of the many investment properties he owned. Much less the details of this castle that had been called the *quiet bedrock of the Tavian brand*, because, yes, the man considered his family a marketing tool and used them that way, too.

Obviously, he had his staff hire more staff to handle all such details and yet more staff to disseminate the myth of his greatness in all things to the wider world in the form of the odd puff piece.

The actual bedrock of the Tavian brand was Umberto's bottomless greed.

Once the car was parked, the usual phalanx of indistinguishable staff members poured out to greet Ivy. They took the small bag she'd brought with her and ushered her inside, pretending to ask after her needs and desires when any guest to this place must know that what really mattered was the way Umberto had decreed they ought to be treated.

Ivy was slightly shocked that she wasn't marched off to the dungeons.

She'd always been convinced that there were dungeons here somewhere. Actual cells, not simply all the mind games that were played here the way some families played a bit of cribbage of an evening.

"You may wait here," a serene-faced woman told Ivy as she led her into a room on the ground floor of the castle, away from the far grander reception rooms and a ballroom as famous for who wasn't invited inside as who was—Umberto did love to make a Hunger Game all his own whenever possible. The woman even bowed her head as she retreated.

None of the staff had looked familiar to Ivy, which didn't surprise her. It wasn't easy to have a personal relationship with an angry, despotic old man who thought he was smarter than anyone he'd ever encountered simply because he was richer. Having to *work* for him had to be nothing short of torturous.

Ivy looked around the room they'd left her in. It was one of the castle's numerous salon-type places because, apparently, outrageously wealthy people got too easily bored with only *one* place to sit. She drifted farther into the room, noting in an almost clinical fashion the pedigreed art on the walls. The sort of antiques that would make a Christie's auctioneer weep. Carefully arranged objects were stacked here and tossed there—because the *suggestion* that the occupants might really come and read all of these books, or might have collected these pieces on some sentimental journey instead of simply buying them because they were sought after by others, was the real truth about what was considered fashionable in houses like this.

But staring at yet another example of Umberto's collection of things quickly lost its appeal.

She drifted over to a series of glass doors that took the place of any outside wall in this room and looked out, expecting to see more bucolic fields brimming with flowers, each competing to be brighter and more riotous than the next.

Instead, she stopped dead.

Because this particular room did not face the vineyards or the fields or the gardens, as expected. This one looked out over a half-shaded terrace that boasted a set of pools. If memory served, each one was set to a different temperature and they were all arranged so that a person could float in any one of them and look out at the landscape as if they were part of it.

Though what she was looking at right this particular moment was not a part of the landscape, for all that it was…primeval.

A man was rising up out of the hot pool, the vapor rising up from the water's surface with him and making it seem as if he, himself, was generating the kind of heat that steamed up a spring morning.

Ivy felt herself freeze. As if her muscles themselves betrayed her, unable to make sense of what she was seeing.

But she couldn't look away.

He rose slowly, climbing up the ladder at the side of the pool with a kind of careless athletic grace that made her head go light. She was half convinced that she'd lapsed off into sleep on one of the self-referential settees inside, suffering from heretofore unknown effects of jet lag from a simple ninety-minute flight from London down into Italy. Because otherwise, she couldn't account for this.

His back was toward her. And yet her mouth went dry as she found her gaze moving over the impossible, powerful shifts of lean muscle beneath golden skin as he lifted himself from the water. He moved up another step and she blinked, because she could suddenly see what had to be the most perfect, bare-naked ass not currently cast in marble and tucked away in a museum that she'd ever beheld.

Still he rose, some kind of ancient god brought to life, as if the old Roman deities had never really disappeared at all. As if he had been here all along, Neptune himself, carved from wonder and sex, water and desire.

He stood at the top of the ladder now and she watched as he speared a powerful hand into his dark hair, currently slicked to shape his skull. A normal, everyday movement that this man—if he was a man and not a figment of her imagination—made into poetry.

Ivy was still frozen solid as if her bones had locked her in place while inside, everything that could soften, melted. And ran hot. She felt as if she was boiling, as if her body couldn't handle this, because what mortal could?

He turned and she saw the rest of him, like the slow dawning of the sun. The wide shoulders, the chest a hagiography of male musculature, more golden skin dusted with dark hair, and all of it arrowing to a narrow waist. And below, a large and heavy cock that did not appear to be reacting to what she imagined were the cooler temperatures outside that hot tub.

Or then again, more worryingly, perhaps this *was* his reaction. Maybe that enormous appendage was, in fact, his shrinkage.

The idea made her entire body break out into goose bumps.

Yet she kept looking. His thighs were powerful, suggesting levels of performance and dedication that she found staggering. But not as staggering as the clear evidence that he did not have a single hint of a tan line. Anywhere.

It was as if he had been created out of Roman gold, dancing sunshine, and pure lust.

Her own breath fogged up the glass window in front of her and Ivy could move then. Suddenly. She found her hand was shaking, but she wiped the fog away.

To find him staring directly at her.

Everything in her froze again. Then seemed to blare back into light and sound and *sensation* with a punch that made her feel as if she had been knocked back across the room. It was a disorienting shock to realize she hadn't moved, but the bigger shock was staring straight at her through the glass.

Ivy knew that face. She knew those dark jade eyes, lit as ever with amusement and mockery. That perfect nose of his that would not look out of place on precious old coins and that cruel mouth that was so often—like now—curled to one side. Derision a certainty.

He stared back at her and she could only imagine what she looked like from his perspective. Panting up a windowed door, clinging to the glass as if it was the only thing keeping her upright.

Oh yes, she knew that face. She knew *him*, for her sins.

She also knew that something terrible had happened in the years since she'd last seen him in the flesh. Because Ivy had known this man since he'd been younger, more obviously feral, all of him somehow *sharper*. His face had been more of a hatchet when he was twenty-two, a deadly object if wielded correctly but more a tool than any weapon.

Now, though he was no less of a blade, that face of his was *honed*. Not the careless sharpness of his youth, but the refinement of his years. Lethal, in other words.

He did absolutely nothing to cover himself, of course. Instead, all he did was stare right back at her as if *she* was the one parading around nude on a bright and sunny April morning in a place where there could be no possible expectation of privacy. He stared at her as if she was the foolish girl she'd been when she'd lived here, always out of her depth and incapable of understanding what was happening all around her—especially if he was involved.

He stared at her and brought back memories of her embarrassing adolescence that she'd thought long-banished to the dustbin of recollections that were no longer welcome now that she was older.

He stared and when she didn't respond, he lifted one dark brow.

Daring her.

Ivy couldn't even have said what it was he was challenging her to do. Not if her life depended on it—and she was dismayed to discover it felt as if it did.

But somehow she managed to wrench herself away, turning back around and retreating from those glass doors as quickly as she could without giving him the satisfaction of seeing her run.

Once she was all the way on the other side of the room, she found that her knees were weak. She had no choice but to lower herself down onto the nearest overtly fussy chair and then had to take a deeply embarrassing inventory of all the ways she was trembling. Shaking. *Goose-bumping* all over. Her heart was pounding so hard it made her feel slightly sick.

And she was slick and hot between her legs, a humiliation from which she was not certain she would ever recover.

She was wrecked, in other words, and she could not understand how any of this was possible.

Because that man was no Roman god. There was nothing the slightest bit holy about him and if there had been at some point he had systematically removed it thanks to his lifelong pursuit of the deepest, darkest depths of any and every vice available.

He was Giaco Tavian. *The* Giaco Tavian.

Once her stepbrother. Always the bane of her existence.

But he was a whole lot more than that, sadly. It was impossible to walk past a single tabloid magazine without seeing his shockingly beautiful face. Not to mention most of that internationally renowned body of his, particularly since he did enjoy spending as much time as possible parading it about. Some years it seemed as if all the yachts in the Mediterranean would sink as one if he were not personally there to keep them afloat with his exploits.

There were a lot of words to describe a man like Giaco. *Lothario. Romeo. Casanova.*

The more modern and less poetic *fuck boy.*

If he was a woman, they simply would have called him a whore.

From a distractingly young age, Giaco Tavian had distinguished himself by being faithless and immoral in every possible respect. His father's only son, and therefore the heir to Umberto's vast empire because Umberto thought his younger daughter was good only for potential gains via marriage, Giaco had used his wealth, privilege, and astonishing good looks to make himself the very embodiment of sin.

In some countries they called him the devil. But that only increased the general appetite for him.

To this day, Giaco remained possibly the most debaucherous creature who had ever swanned his way in and out of the bedrooms of Europe, which he did with such regularity that some theorized—without hyperbole—that he might possibly have *actually* slept with *everybody.* He was a scandal in a distractingly beautiful male form that she had now experienced personally.

Even though she had previously been gloriously immune.

Ivy didn't understand how this was possible, and no matter that she could still feel her own body's betrayal. She had always loathed Giaco. His smoldering about. His utter disregard for the feelings of absolutely everything and everyone he encountered. His obvious pleasure in making as many people around him as uncomfortable as possible. He made alley cats seem like monks. He was pathologically boneless, confronting, and deeply comfortable with the outrage that followed him around like his baying packs of adoring would-be lovers.

He was a very particular kind of fantasy made flesh, there was no denying it. Yet how he could possibly have emerged from the loins of his father, who Ivy had always thought of—without a shred of affection—as the Lizard King, she could not imagine.

It was likely a gift from his Persian mother, another renowned beauty who had been lost too soon—no doubt to the same neglect that had destroyed Ivy's mother. Because one thing about Umberto was that he did like to collect beautiful women and then destroy them. If he had a leisure activity, it was that.

Ivy blew out a breath, happy to feel that her heart was slowing down a bit. That she was getting back to normal. She needed the reminder she wasn't here for...whatever that was that had just happened. Giaco was nothing if not a distraction. She was fairly certain that was his entire purpose in life. But his nonsense had nothing to do with her.

She made her breath even and tried to make herself relax. She hadn't expected to see her former stepbrother today. She certainly hadn't expected to see *so much* of him. But the more she thought about it, the more she decided it was like diving straight off the high dive into deep water, and probably good for her.

It could only benefit her to remember who she was dealing with and why.

Ivy thought of her own mother then. The world-renowned Alana Amis, who had been so beautiful that men had fallen over in the street at the sight of her, yet had carried around an insecurity that far outstripped her looks or her accomplishments or the simple, joyful person she could be when no one was looking. Her lovely and wildly talented mother, who was so luminous on-screen that a single tear from her could make audiences sob for days and who, despite all her fame and her enduring legend, had wanted only the simplest of things in the end.

To be loved. To be taken care of. To matter to someone.

Ivy would never forgive her stepfather for failing Alana on each and every point.

The door opened. Her eyes snapped open, her heart kicked at her again, and she was certain that she was about to see even more of Giaco Tavian. But instead, it was another member of the staff. He beckoned for her to follow him and then led her farther into the castle, to deliver her to what she knew was Umberto's private office.

She walked inside and found the stepfather she had never intended to see again looking as if he was relaxing—a sure sign that this was going to be a bit of blood sport on his end. Nothing about Umberto Tavian was leisurely, and yet today he was sitting in a chair in one of the seating areas that dotted the large room with a drink in his hand and his usual heavy-lidded, contemptuous look in his eyes.

"What a marvelous surprise," he said, speaking English as if he thought Ivy was perhaps not fluent in it. Or, more likely, as if he assumed she was simply dim-witted. See: the silly, foolish, idiotic girl he thought she was. "You were so certain that you would never return to the fold, Ivy. And yet here you are. Just as I knew you would be, one day."

The Ivy she'd been when she'd left this place five years ago, having just buried her mother and vowing never to return, would have told him where he could shove that. With malice and pleasure.

But she'd gotten smarter, these past years. More strategic. There were things that mattered a whole lot more to her than attempting to land a blow on a man like Umberto when she knew perfectly well that he felt nothing. She supposed he was amply insulated not only by the rich food he preferred and the indulgent, debaucherous lifestyle he exulted in, but by all the money he'd extracted from every business enterprise he'd ever touched.

He called himself a *financier*.

But she knew that he preferred to play kingmaker. Regime toppler, if given the chance, because he liked a show. He had his thick, fleshy fingers in every possible pot and sat here in his castle like a big, round spider, casting his webs far and wide.

Young Ivy had felt smothered and claustrophobic and had dealt with that by lashing out, which had garnered her precisely nothing. But she'd learned from that.

Today she simply walked in, kept smiling at him no matter what he said or what tone he used, and took a seat in the chair opposite his.

"I don't want to take up too much of your time," she said, politely. She'd learned that, too. The clever art of conversation with unpleasant people. She'd spent years figuring out how to use her status as a well-known nepo baby to get done the kinds of things that needed doing, in her view. She'd spent years learning how to shine brightly for men like this, because that was the only way to get them to part with their money.

And Ivy loved nothing more than a man who could be flattered into giving large donations to her charity. The orphans didn't care how she got that money. They only benefited when she had it. It was her job to make sure she had as much as possible at all times.

"Yes, yes," Umberto was saying. He swirled his drink in its tumbler. "You are here for your little fortune, I know."

One of the interesting things about the way she'd spent the last five years of life was that Ivy knew a whole lot more people now. Many of them from entirely different walks of life than the one she'd grown up in. Her *little fortune*, as Umberto called it, was easily millions of pounds. Part of it was the money that her mother had inherited upon Ivy's father's death. He too had been an actor—but before that, he'd been born into the English aristocracy. Add to that the numerous fortunes her mother had made as a screen legend and no reasonable person would call her inheritance *a little fortune*.

But of course, to a man like this, it was nothing.

Ivy swallowed back her fury, the rest of the emotions this place and this awful man stirred up in her, and everything else she felt but did not wish to feel while she was subjecting herself to this game of his. Even the walls themselves were unsafe in Umberto's private castle. No doubt plastered over a hundred times with the indifference this man had shown every person he'd ever brought here. Her mother included.

Her mother was the reason she was here. Her mother

and what her help from beyond the grave could do for innumerable children in need.

"The funds my mother left me, yes," she agreed, still with a polite smile. She had practiced and practiced, knowing that it would be difficult not to snarl at this man. It turned out it was even harder than anticipated.

Umberto nodded as if she was a small, precocious child who'd learned a big word. "I will help you with this, my dear."

Ivy had to fight not to vomit. *My dear.* What a vile man he was. He knew she hated him. Got off on it, if she had to guess.

But, "Thank you," was all she said, as if she thought he was sincere.

Because what else was there to say? Her mother had made Umberto the executor of Ivy's inheritance. Ivy had some theories about how that had come to pass, most of them having to do with Umberto's controlling tendencies, but that didn't change the fact that she could not access that money without him signing off on it.

She had decided years ago that she would rather turn her back on her inheritance than subject herself to the kind of performative obeisance with too many strings to count that she knew Umberto would demand.

But times had changed. More importantly, her needs had changed. If this had been just about her, she never would have come back here. She would rather prostitute herself on the streets of London than demean herself for this man's amusement. It had been clear from the moment he'd accepted her call that Umberto would make her jump through hoops once she'd come crawling back and that she would hate every moment of it.

Lucky, then, that this wasn't about how she *felt*.

"I'm an old man," Umberto told her, with a smug look on his face, because men like him didn't really believe they were old. Not the way other men were old. Men like Umberto didn't believe that being old made *them* weak the way it did others. They were so sure their wealth and consequence made them *better*. "My only joys in this life come from my business dealings and I have on the table a particularly exciting deal. I won't bore you with the details. Pretty girls have much better things to think about, I'm sure."

Ivy gritted her teeth, kept her smile on her face, and wondered—not for the first time—what it was like to be poor Leontina, Umberto's usually wholly ignored daughter. She remembered her former stepsister as little more than a shadow in the corner, which had always struck her as odd when the two of them weren't far apart in age. But then, she supposed that was an answer in and of itself.

"But in order for this deal to go through, I'm afraid there is a challenge that I must overcome," Umberto continued. "There's a moral stipulation, you understand."

Ivy did not understand. She also didn't care. So she nodded, trying to look as if she was actively listening to this.

Umberto smiled. Always chilling. "As you are no doubt aware, *moral* is not a word that has ever been applied to my son."

That got her attention. Or rather, the sight of Giaco rising from the steaming water came back to her like a punch to the gut. She coughed into her fist, cleared her throat, and nodded. "I can't say I've kept up with him in all these years," she lied.

Well. It wasn't really a lie, was it? She hadn't kept up with him in the sense that she hadn't privately considered him at all. But he was inescapable. The legend of Giaco Tavian was an international preoccupation. His collections of lovers. Their breathless tales of his prowess. The not-so-subtle hints of his sexual deviance, his penchant for bedroom games, his wholly indiscriminate selection processes, and the high-octane, jet-setting, partying lifestyle that went along with all of that.

Umberto didn't seem to care if she was prepared to admit the omnipresence of his son's sins or not. "When you called I realized that there was a simple, elegant solution. I've watched what you've done with yourself over the years, Ivy. It's hard to imagine that such a spoiled, petulant girl could turn into the toast of London, but you've managed it."

The Lizard King never blinked when he was busy handing out insults, and this was no exception. He watched her, clearly expecting her to react to his characterization of her adolescent behavior while trapped in his clutches.

Instead, she smiled and said, "I've been lucky enough to make great friends in London. I suppose we all have the places where we truly shine, don't we?"

Umberto made a scoffing noise. "I don't know about *shining*," he said. "But most people in your situation, considered celebrities thanks to having been adjacent to the fame of others, follow a different trajectory. Yet you, by all accounts, are a living saint. Lady Bountiful herself, friend to orphan children, bestowing her kindness as best she can. Truly, a heartwarming tale to inspire the most cynical heart."

He neither looked nor sounded the slightest bit inspired.

"I found myself orphaned five years ago, when I was twenty, and it was shockingly disorienting," Ivy began calmly, as this was a story she had told many times before. "It made me wonder how much worse it must be for those who do not have my advantages, or my—"

"I've heard these little speeches," Umberto interrupted her, sounding bored. "It's why I brought you here. No one is more astonished than me, given the path I expected you would take when you left here, but you have made yourself a reputation for moral fortitude. And as it happens, I need it."

For a moment, the way he looked at her, Ivy had a creeping, *horrifying* notion take her over. Umberto was forever marrying trophies. Surely he didn't think her *moral fortitude*, whatever the hell that was, qualified? She would climb to the top of his castle and fling herself off it first.

Instead, Umberto reached over and rang the bell beside him, then nodded when one of his servants opened the door. "Bring him in," he said, a crisp order.

And moments later, Giaco himself ambled in. He was not dressed. He had covered himself with a silk robe, but that was his only nod to civility.

Ivy could not bear to look at him any more than she already had today, especially not when his gaze found hers as he entered and lit up at once with that unholy amusement of his. Instead, she watched Umberto and found herself nothing short of delighted to see that Giaco got to him, too. The old man was fairly bristling.

She had always enjoyed how easily riled he was. This

man who fancied himself the king above all kings could not tolerate the faintest poke in his direction, and Ivy dearly wished that she was in a place where she could deliver a few such pokes.

It was almost better, however, that it was Giaco. Since his existence, for all intents and purposes, was the greatest and most effective poke at Umberto possible.

"Is there some reason you are not dressed?" Umberto growled at his son and heir.

"I prefer not to dress at all," Giaco replied, in that lazy drawl of his. No matter what language he was speaking, he always sounded as if vocabulary itself made him sleepy. As if he needed to taste every word as it came out of his mouth, and that required all his energy. "I'm happy to remove this robe, father. Would you like that?"

Umberto made a growling sound. If Ivy didn't dislike Giaco so much herself, she might have applauded.

Then it was impossible not to watch as Giaco took his time sauntering over to the couch that stretched between her chair and Umberto's and flung himself down upon it. With no particular attention paid to whether or not his robe would cover him.

That it did was a miracle.

But even as Ivy thought that, she found him watching her, the dark jade of gaze mocking. Because he knew— somehow he *knew*—that she was thinking of exactly what he had beneath the fabric of his robe. He probably knew that she had committed it all to memory, damn him.

She felt herself *heat* and hated him. Hard. Then tried to focus on his loathsome father instead.

Umberto threw back the remains of his drink. "In

order to close this deal, and I am determined to close it, I am afraid that the tawdry legend of Giaco Tavian, heralded cocksman, must come to an ignominious end."

"Must it?" Giaco asked, sounding bored. "But I am so popular and beloved as is. Ask anyone."

"This is what will happen," Umberto said curtly. "The two of you will engage upon a relationship. It will be widely photographed. A worldwide love affair, focusing on Ivy's rather impressive virtue and not the fact that she was once a stepsister. Finally, they all will declare, a woman who tames the savage beast—and whatever other maudlin story the papers choose to tell. You will see to it."

Ivy could not comprehend anything the demented old man was saying. She could not make any of those words make sense, much less *together*.

Giaco sighed, sounding even more bored and now amused besides. "And why would I do that?"

"Because if you do not, I will cut you off entirely," Umberto told him. "And I doubt very much that you have any skills outside your preferred bedsport, Giaco. Given that you have never exhibited the slightest inclination toward anything else."

Giaco shrugged, lying there on his back on the sofa as if about to drop off into a nap at any moment. "Fair point."

"There will be an engagement. The world will go wild. It will seem inevitable—fated, even—that the only woman capable of civilizing such a beast is the one who grew up in this house and thus learned the secrets of Giaco's benighted soul, whatever they might be. Again, the press will be encouraged to pursue the *virtue*. The *romance*. There will be no scandal. There will be no *dark intimations* about what you got up to with her when she was an adolescent."

"Father," Giaco said then, in mock astonishment. "I had no idea that you cared what anyone got up to, as an adolescent or otherwise. Or that such a romantic has lurked within you all this time."

Ivy found this significantly less amusing than Giaco seemed to. Yet she still couldn't bring herself to speak.

"And then, the coup de grâce," Umberto said, with deep satisfaction and what looked a lot like actual malice, to Ivy's eye. "You will marry. It goes without saying that during the period of this whirlwind romance and into your marriage, which will last for at least three years, there will be absolutely nothing but squeaky-clean behavior. More virtue. So much virtue that canonization will seem inevitable. Your transformation, Giaco, will be a thing of epic beauty or you will pay for it. Meanwhile, my deal *will* go through and it *will* survive its probationary period. Then I will wash my hands of the both of you and happily pay to never think of either one of you again."

Ivy couldn't breathe. She didn't know where to look. It was bad enough that she'd seen *all* of Giaco today. Now she was supposed to… Date him? Pretend to fall in love with him? She was not an actress. She was only related to a late, legendary one and had not inherited the faintest shred of Alana's talent. How would any of this work?

She found herself drawn to look at him again, telling herself it was the horror of this that was making her seek him out for some kind of confirmation that he was hearing the same things she was.

But all she saw was that too-dark jade, so mocking, and currently filled with what looked like some kind of glee.

"For you, Father, anything—if it affects my bank accounts. I'm sure that sweet, virtuous, stepsister Ivy and I can work it out," Giaco said, though that gaze of his was fastened to Ivy, and there was nothing about it that suggested he saw her as *sweet* or virtuous in any way. "As long as you're aware, my soon-to-be beloved and bride, that I require a not inconsiderable amount of fucking. Daily. Can you handle that?"

CHAPTER TWO

Giaco Tavian had long ago made his life into performance art, the more outrageous and inaccessible to the observer, the better.

Also, he did indeed enjoy a good daily fuck.

But never had he enjoyed himself more than he did right now. He had assumed that his objectively hideous father was cooking up some or other unfortunate plan—because Umberto was always so busy with all his plotting that Giaco assumed it was what kept him alive—when the old man had summoned him home to the family castle. Particularly when he'd insisted rather darkly that it was Giaco's turn to *pay the piper*.

He had been tempted to ask his father what, if any, experience Umberto himself had with pipers of any description. Because Giaco knew that the old man was the sort who believed that he could buy himself out of any situation. And frequently did. No pipers requiring payment. None to lead blind mice. It was a piper-free existence for a man so corrupt he made the crime families all over Italy seem virtuous in comparison.

But Giaco was nothing if not committed to the role he played. To finding a new low in everything he did.

Though he had to admit that looking up from a morning dip to find his former stepsister ogling him was really more of a high.

Especially because Ivy hadn't been anything like *this* attractive when she'd lived here. He'd barely noticed her, appropriately, as she was a good ten years younger than him. He had been in his early twenties and had only returned to the castle for his monthly sessions with his father, wherein Umberto had made him perform for his monthly stipend. Luckily, Giaco had discovered long before that all he really needed to do was disgust the old man with tales of his exploits. The monthly meetings had been discontinued at some point in his twenties.

These days Giaco preferred that his father read about his exploits in various papers or hear about them from his business associates. He dedicated himself to this task for many reasons, one of them being that Umberto thrived in the murkiest of shadows. Umberto was the sort who liked to hide behind a throne because kings came and went, but men like Umberto always remained.

Giaco liked to think of himself as a bright bit of sun—a spotlight, if you would—that shone upon Umberto wherever he went. Umberto had usually sent him off again in a fury, stipend dispensed, just to get Giaco out of his sight.

If Giaco had seen Ivy over the course of those years, she had made no impression on him.

That had changed in that last year, when her mother was ill. He had noticed her then. She had grown into her angular face, he could remember thinking. And she had looked far too pretty next to her mother's coffin, an observation even he had known to keep to himself.

But he couldn't say he'd thought much of her or about her since.

The Ivy who had turned up today and who had watched him like he was her favorite dirty movie, on the other hand, was a surprise.

And Giaco could not remember the last time that he been even remotely surprised. By anything.

He scoured his memory for hints of her when she was younger, but all he could pull up were vague impressions of the adolescent version of her—the odd glimpse of blond hair and a sullen expression.

That had changed when he'd seen her at her mother's funeral. And also before it, if he recalled correctly, when he'd allowed an overeager acolyte to pleasure him and had looked up from the bench he'd been lounging on—just before the woman in question was about to busy herself with him—and had seen Ivy loitering about in the doorway.

There had been a look on her face, however briefly, that had…made the situation far hotter than a desultory bit of oral usually was.

Today Ivy did not have grief in her eyes. She looked polished to a gleam. She was still blond, though today all of that blond hair was pulled back into a sleek sort of ponytail that looked effortless and had therefore likely taken hours to perfect. She had impossibly, distractingly blue eyes. A different sort of man might have been tempted to compare them to summer skies or the deep blue sea. Giaco was more interested in the way they appeared to be clear, yet were unreadable.

Not what she seemed, then, was Ivy. That was intriguing.

Her mother had been a great, rare beauty. Giaco could see Alana Amis's famous influence in the exquisite bone structure of Ivy's face. In her aquiline nose and wide, offhandedly sensual mouth. She looked like one of those women who heaved about on those recovery machines and called it a workout, then attributed their lithe forms to the practice when it was clearly just genetics.

In Ivy's case it was *excellent* genetics. He had no idea if she'd ever taken a Pilates class in her life, but he knew where she'd gotten that inherent elegance she wore so easily.

Here in his father's office, which had all the aesthetic appeal of a prison, she looked cool. Unruffled. She wore slim-fitting jeans, flats, and a simple sweater, but the cut of each of those items was exquisite. There was the hint of diamond sparkle in her ears and single pearl drop around her neck.

Giaco knew battle armor when he saw it.

More telling, to his mind, was that she had said absolutely nothing since his father's announcement.

"You seem undone," he pointed out, pillowing his head on his folded arms. He shifted his legs, entertained by the way his father huffed and looked away and Ivy dropped her gaze. Both of them expecting to see him, cock out, on the sofa.

He did not intend to let them realize that he was wearing boxer briefs. What fun would that be?

Ivy still didn't answer, so he lifted his brow. "Is it the acting job for such a wide audience that you find unappealing? Or is it the daily fucking that, it has to be said, a great many people do insist is excessive. I'm afraid I run at a higher intensity than some."

"You will stop using that word," his father growled.

"I know this is distressing, father," Giaco said, so pleasantly he should have been smiling ear to ear. He wasn't. "But I am, despite all protestations to the contrary, a fully grown adult. And will use whatever vocabulary I please."

"I'm going to take this opportunity to make it clear that I don't care who or what you fuck," Ivy announced in that British accent of hers that made her vowels gleam like polished glass. "That has nothing to do with me. If this is the only way that I can receive my inheritance, I suppose I will have to find a way to channel my mother's gifts and pretend that when I look at you I feel nothing but adoration. Instead of the more natural revulsion."

"Revulsion?" Giaco smirked at her. "Are we certain that's what it is?"

And he was more pleased than he probably should have been to see the hint of color on her cheeks.

His father stood in a rush then, likely because this was no longer about him.

"I want to read about the two of you in the papers as soon as possible and I don't care how you do it." Umberto glared at his only son and heir. "I know perfectly well that you have contacts among the paparazzi. Sell the story I want to read, Giaco. Your total redemption at the hands of the sort of saintly female you would normally take such pleasure in befouling, etcetera, etcetera. Or you will wish you had."

"Dearest Papà, I have never experienced a moment of regret in my life," Giaco murmured. "I wouldn't recognize it if I did."

His father sneered. "You will recognize it, Giaco. This I promise you."

And then Umberto stormed on out of the room, no doubt off to smite down some enemies and ruin more lives. It was his favorite pastime. And possibly his only pastime.

Giaco did not move. He did not allow himself to think too deeply about what was actually happening here, beneath the surface, because there was no point in it at this stage. He watched Ivy instead.

"I'm surprised that you allow him to threaten you," she said after a moment. "It doesn't really seem to go with your whole…" She waved a hand. "Aesthetic."

That interested him against his will. He actually sat up and let the robe fall open as he did. He watched her jolt a little bit, hide it, and then release a breath when she saw that he was covered after all.

Most people did not pay enough attention to Giaco. Oh, they paid attention to the stories. To the spotlight that followed him wherever he went. To all the smoke and mirrors and the outrageousness he threw about like so much confetti.

But if there was tension between how he behaved and how he was *thought* to behave, or any question of aesthetics or intentions or anything else that didn't match—well, that wasn't the sort of thing people thought about when it came to him. No one thought Umberto's useless son was bright enough to know what he was doing.

He counted on that.

"And have you studied my aesthetic at great length, then?" he asked Ivy. "I am fascinating, it is true. There are many who have engaged in a doctoral level of research into the topic. Is that why you came back?"

"You know why I came back." She blew out a breath. "Or maybe you don't. My mother left me money. It's my money. A normal person would have given it me according to her wishes five years ago, but, of course, we're talking about your father."

"Your first impulse was the better one," he told her, making sure to sound idle and bored. His specialty. Even though he meant it. Maybe especially because he meant it. "Nothing good ever comes of succumbing to my father's wishes."

Ivy laughed. "Who do you think you're telling? I watched him catch my mother in his nasty little net, pull off her wings, and pin her down. She was never the same. He took everything that was good and sure about her and destroyed it. Because he could." She shook her head, her mouth firming. "That's the part that I keep coming back to. It would have been one thing if he had actually had malicious intent toward her. But I don't think he did, and that's worse."

"The only things my father cares about are money and power," Giaco said. "He's like a dragon with a horde."

Ivy nodded. "I always called him the Lizard King. Sadly not to his face."

He laughed at that, surprising himself. "Just so."

Ivy stood up from her chair and he watched, fascinated, as she…paced across the stone floor. She even fidgeted, using her thumb and forefinger to pull at her bottom lip—quite absently, he was sure. He could tell.

Giaco had a sudden, perfectly formed image in his head—almost as if it was a memory, when it wasn't, of course it wasn't—of nipping the place her fingers touched as he lifted her up and then lowered her onto his cock—

Settle down, he told himself sharply. This was business.

"How does this work?" she asked abruptly, frowning at him as if he was a clerk who was holding on to information he required. Or a secretary of some kind. All efficient practicality.

It was true that this was business, but Giaco was not used to beautiful women behaving this way in his presence. They tended to…flutter. Melt. There was a lot of helpless giggling, melting gazes, sultry smiles.

A lot like the way she'd looked when she'd seen him by the pool.

But then, he was quite certain she hadn't realized it was him at first.

That would be a lowering thought, but it was difficult for Giaco to achieve a lower place than the one he inhabited. So he shrugged it off.

"It's very simple," he told her. "Though perhaps less so for the officiously virtuous. When a man and a woman like each other, sometimes they pull off all of their clothes and roll around together—"

Her blue gaze was withering. "Your father seems to think that you can mount a publicity campaign with a snap of your fingers. Is that true?"

"It is less a snap of my fingers and more a few well-placed texts," he acknowledged. "But it is true that the papers and I have a kind of symbiotic relationship."

"Right." She looked at him, as if studying his face for flaws. He knew that there were none. Yet, oddly enough, he found himself sitting just the slightest bit straighter all the same. He watched her as she clearly came to a decision. "I'll go along with this because I think the ends justify the means. I'm still not clear why you would do the same, though. As far as I know, you've never done a single thing your father ever asked of you."

"I have dedicated myself to disappointing him, it is true," Giaco agreed with a sigh. "But into every man's life a shadow must fall. I'm afraid that I have no option but to obey him in this."

She did not look convinced. Giaco took that as something of a compliment.

"Obey?" she asked after a moment. "This is something you do?"

He smiled. "Only if it benefits me."

Giaco stretched out one arm over the back of the sofa and lounged there, fully aware—almost too aware, to his mind—of the way her gaze kept lowering to his bare torso. She would look down, then her gaze would flick up again. More than once. And all the while, the color on her cheeks intensified.

Interesting.

"Forgive me," she said with a smile. A practiced smile, he thought. He knew one when he saw it. "I don't pretend to know you. That's never been of the slightest interest to me, or to you, I'm sure. Yet I can't help thinking that you have ulterior motives here."

"But surely that is impossible," he drawled. "I'm empty-headed. Merely a dissipated, pleasure-seeking fool, forever at the mercy of my constantly changing passions. An ulterior motive sounds like work."

"And yet I need to be assured that if I start down this

road with you, it won't blow up in my face." She eyed him with a little too much of that practicality and efficiency then. "I don't care what you do with your life, Giaco. What I do care about is mine."

He waved a hand. "Did you run out of your money already? It happens to the best of us."

"I have plenty of money," she retorted. "But the orphan's charity that I run does not."

He threw his head back at that and her prim, outraged expression, and laughed. "I didn't realize I was in the presence of an *actual* saint. I do not typically run into such virtue, you understand. To me it merely looks like self-flagellation."

"Charity seems like self-flagellation?" She let out her own laugh at that, though hers was more brittle. "That doesn't even make sense."

"I don't believe in charity," he said, mostly so that he could see her bristle. "Unless you mean in a sexual sense."

She blinked. "I...absolutely do not mean it in that sense. I don't think I want to know what that means to you. Really."

"I would be happy to tell you, Ivy. *Stepsister.* You need only ask."

"What I'd like you to tell me, person with no relationship to me at all, is how you intend to make this thing work to your father's satisfaction. All the rest of it? All of these games you like to play?" She shook her head, her gaze cool. "I don't want any part of that. I find the way that you slink about as if you might spontaneously burst into an orgasm repulsive in the extreme."

He threw back his head and laughed at that, too. Then

sobered as he watched her look down the length of him, then up, then flush again. "I don't think that you do."

"I fear that says more about your powers of observation than anything else."

"This puts us in a bind," he said, heaving a sigh and making it sound sorrowful. Vaguely. "Because if you and I cannot work up some believable chemistry, I'm afraid you'll have to go back, hair shirt and penitent cross in hand as I assume one so holy does, to apologize to your poor orphans for failing them."

She looked…mutinous. Possibly enraged, though he doubted she would unbend enough to be *truly* angry. Certainly not in public.

She folded her arms and glared at him. "I don't think chemistry is the issue."

"Chemistry is almost always the issue," he assured her. "But indulge me. What do *you* think the issue is?"

"You," she replied flatly. "No one will ever believe that any woman could possibly settle you down."

"You need to believe in yourself more," he suggested. "I think there are meditation retreats for that. A whole lot of heaving about, concerned with breathing and unattractive yogic poses. At the end you'll come back a new woman. All you have to do is pay an obscene amount of money to sleep on the floor and eat plain, uninspiring food and perhaps scrub a few floors and windows, all in the company of bored socialites just like you."

She blinked. "What sort of meditation retreats have you attended? That sounds like a work camp. Were you perhaps incarcerated without your realizing it?"

Giaco shrugged. "That is entirely possible."

"In any case, it has nothing to do with me," she continued. "You're completely unbelievable as a romantic lead. No one who has ever heard of you—and sadly, everyone has heard of you, against their will—would ever believe that you would date only one person, much less propose to her. And it absolutely beggars belief that you would ever marry."

"A stinging indictment indeed," he murmured. Then lifted a shoulder. "But you forget that the camera loves me. It will show the world precisely what I wish it to, never you fear."

"But I do fear," Ivy said. "I don't believe it's possible."

"Well," he replied, with a theatrical sort of sigh. "If you insist, I'll be happy to give a demonstration."

She only stared back at him, and he sighed again. So put upon. So beleaguered, as he lounged about half-undressed in the company of a beautiful woman that he was going to marry, and likely soon.

Giaco lifted a hand and beckoned her to him with two fingers. "Come on, then. Come here, little saint. Let's see if I can make you believe that your virtue has redeemed me."

CHAPTER THREE

THE WILDEST PART was that Ivy actually wanted to do it. Or if she didn't *want* it, necessarily, there was something inside her that was urging her on. A kind of *tugging* she'd never felt before in her life. Like there was a band of *need* wrapped tight around the very center of her, pulling her toward him.

She didn't understand it at all.

Logically, it made no sense. She knew exactly who Giaco was, for her sins. She knew what he did. How he did it, even. She'd spent years witnessing the chaos and carnage he left in his wake every time he visited his family, usually in the form of Umberto's temper tantrums after his departure that the old man doled out indiscriminately and with a certain relish, to Ivy's mind. And in case she'd been predisposed to think that was a family issue, the unavoidable tabloid coverage of Giaco made it more than clear that such upheaval was his raison d'être wherever he happened to find himself.

Ivy'd had something of a run-in with him five years ago in the run-up to her mother's funeral, those hazy, heavy days while the arrangements were being made by the very people who hadn't cared about Alana while she'd been alive. Ivy had been…raw. And she'd stumbled across Giaco in one of the castle galleries, flirting out-rageously with a woman Ivy hadn't recognized. Maybe she'd been one of the mourners who had been there less because they cared at all about Ivy's mother and more because they thought Alana's death meant they were in with a chance with Umberto.

Ivy had been all of twenty years old, more sheltered than she would have admitted at the time, and yet had still been perfectly aware that had she come a few moments later, that woman would likely have been kneeling between Giaco's legs as he lounged back on one of the viewing benches.

She had already been hovering there, knees bent, as if in mid-kneel.

Giaco had looked over lazily. He'd seen Ivy standing there and had only shrugged. Clearly not caring if she stayed or went.

She had, obviously, turned right around and gotten out of there.

Yet for some reason, it had taken her longer than it should have to forget about that moment. She supposed the trauma of her mother's actual funeral hadn't helped, because what she remembered now were all the times she'd had flashes of that expression on his face after-ward. For far too long after she'd escaped this place and made her way back to London.

Happily, it had gone away. And she really didn't know why she was remembering it again now.

Or why she could feel something deep within her kindle into an odd little flame as she stood there, as if she too felt that same voracious *need* she'd watched in an-other woman years ago. To kneel before him. To place herself between those carelessly outspread legs. To gaze up at him, tilt her face toward him, and—

Good God, she thought. The man was like a drug. The sort that came with dire warnings and distressing media campaigns.

And now he wanted to make her believe that *her* virtue had redeemed *him*?

"I will be doing absolutely nothing of the kind," Ivy told him, and she was aware that she sounded more prim and proper than she'd ever felt a day in her life. But for some reason it seemed like a defense. Yet he only gazed back at her, too much dark jade and that curve to his impossible mouth. She huffed out a breath. "I don't need to prove anything to you. In fact, the more I think about it, the more I think it makes sense that my reactions to you should be organic. After all, if this ridiculous performance is to be believed, it would make sense that you would have to do more convincing than me. No sane, reasonable woman, virtuous or not, would ever wish to be seen in your presence. Much less imagine that she could *date* and then *marry* you."

It was so absurd that she laughed.

But Giaco only inclined his head as if she'd complimented him. "It is true that I am a movable feast, indeed. Hemingway would be so proud."

Ivy did not want to think too much about how or why *this* man of all men was making literary references. It was one more thing that made no sense. "You still haven't told me how this is all going to work," she said instead, briskly. "Do you just wave a magic wand? And lo, fawning members of the press appear before you?"

He looked amused, and not in that sharp, painful way

he often did. "More or less. Sometimes I simply step outside."

"You should text them, then." It sounded like she was giving him orders, and she could tell he wasn't used to that in the way his dark brows rose. Ivy decided to take that as a sign she was on the right path. "Once you sort it out, you can tell me where to meet you and what sort of date it is so I can turn myself out appropriately, and we'll get this moving."

"Stop," he murmured. "This is so scandalous. You're making me blush."

Ivy realized that she could continue to stand there, fighting her own body's bizarre response to him, or she could act as if this was all settled. Because it should have been settled. She chose the latter, so she nodded at him and then started for the door.

"Now, now, little saint," Giaco said, sounding...decadent and lush, somehow. "Don't be in such a rush. We have so many things left to discuss."

"I'm happy to have a discussion." She stopped walking and looked back over her shoulder at him. "All you seem to want to do is muddle around in all your innuendo. It's boring. If we're not going to have a practical conversation about the way this is going to work, I don't see the point of it. You can go ahead and email me your thoughts, or whatever schedule you come up with, hopefully without all the smirking and the sighing and this endless performance you like to put on."

She didn't really mean to say that the way that she did, so forcefully. But she wasn't sorry she'd done it that way when she saw his reaction. Oh, it was small. Almost unnoticeable. But something about that perfect face of his changed. Just for a moment.

But Ivy saw it.

Unless she was very much mistaken, she had landed a significant blow.

The trouble was, she just couldn't imagine *how*.

"I had no idea you were so stern and dominating," he murmured in that idle, yet richly tenored way of his. "How delicious." He crooked a finger at her, watching her intently. When Ivy made no move toward him, he sighed a little—yet not with the histrionics from before, so she supposed she ought to have been grateful for small mercies. He patted the sofa seat beside him, and she felt... less grateful. "We're about to become famous lovers, Ivy. The very least we ought to do is exchange mobile numbers. Not to mention that email address I'll need to contact you as you have demanded. I do so enjoy obedience, as I mentioned."

"When it benefits you," she replied, parroting what he'd told her.

His dark eyes gleamed. "Indeed."

She felt as if she was something small and fluttery, caught in a trap. Or possibly between his hands.

And the thought of that, of being held between his palms, didn't actually do anything to steady her breathing. Much less sort out whatever was going on with her heartbeat.

All she could see when she looked at him was danger.

But if they were really going to do what Umberto wanted them to do, Ivy didn't see that she had any choice when it came to dealing with him. And since she didn't have a choice, it made sense to treat him the way she intended to go on.

Meaning she couldn't let him set the tone. She couldn't let him control everything.

She *really* couldn't let him think that she was intimidated by him. She was fully aware that he wanted her to be. That he *expected* her to be.

Maybe he remembered her scuttling off from that gallery, too.

Ivy made herself walk back across the room and sit down next to him on that couch, even though every iota of self-preservation she had within her was telling her to run in the opposite direction. Like the little mouse he made her feel like she was.

She might *feel* like one, Ivy counseled herself, but he didn't need to know that.

It was just an unfortunate fact of life that even sitting on a separate sofa cushion from the man was too close. She could *smell* him. And it was an outrageously pleasant scent. She told herself it must be some kind of aftershave, though if so, she had never smelled anything like it. He just smelled…good. The way sunshine would smell if it had a scent.

It made her think of the few blissful holidays she'd taken in her time, her face tipped up to the sun, all of that heat and ease—

Somehow, she schooled her expression to something impassive and gazed back at him, ordering herself to stop with all the *sunshine*.

Giaco watched her closely, and Ivy wondered how it was that he'd convinced the entire world that he was nothing but a pageant of indolence. When she could see that he was studying her intently, like he was taking the pieces of her and examining them.

Almost like some kind of bird of prey. As if he could see every single thought that scrolled across her mind. In flashing neon lights.

This took significantly more attention to detail than a professional playboy like Giaco Tavian had ever been imagined to possess. It was also the last thing she wanted.

He shifted in his seat, his outstretched arm curling in so he could prop up his head with his own hand. As if the mere act of talking with her was exhausting. Ivy had never beheld such a lazy creature in all her life—except that, too, didn't make any sense.

She had inspected his naked body earlier, against her will and frozen into place. And while it was possible that genetics played a role in his physique, no one could maintain *all that* without effort. She knew that people liked to believe that it was possible. That some humans simply wafted around, treated their bodies horrendously, and were naturally gorgeous and fit and lovely anyway. Or were chemically made that way because they could afford to fix whatever they broke. And there were certain physiques that could come as a natural result of partying, or as a result of cleaning up after said partying, but his wasn't one of them.

Those muscles of his required *work*.

Which meant that all of this was a charade. A long-term, very deliberate game.

Ivy was going to have to think about what that meant.

But not now, because she needed all her wits about her to deal with the *fact* of him sitting there entirely too close to her, regarding her with those dark jade eyes that should not have been as affecting as they were. From afar, they were arresting. The tragedy was, up close, they were even more mesmerizing. They were shot through with hints of gold, but it was a dark gold. As if a treasure reserved only for those who truly saw him.

She couldn't believe she'd actually had that thought. But the good news was, it was so inappropriate and off the chain it was galvanizing.

"Right," she said briskly, sitting much too straight on the cushion next to his. "I could do with less *gazing*, if you don't mind. It's not really productive."

That curve in his mouth deepened, a lot like he was *tasting* this moment—another unnecessary thought. "I have certainly never been accused of being productive."

She pulled out her phone, opened the screen, and handed it over to him when she pulled up the phone pad. "Call yourself," she ordered him.

Brusquely.

"I live to serve," he replied merrily, though she could hear that sardonic undertone.

She decided she didn't care about his undertones. Just as long as he did what was necessary. For a moment, she wasn't sure that he would—

But after a pause, Giaco took the phone from her. And he also let their fingers brush as he did it. Maybe they simply brushed against each other because they were close. She wasn't sure she should ascribe that much intention to the things he did, no matter what she thought she saw when she was this close to him.

Either way, she felt the spark of that touch race through her body. It was alarming.

It felt a great deal like the way she'd had narcotics explained to her. A wild burst of euphoria followed by heat.

It took everything she had not to jerk back as if she'd received an electric shock. When she was pretty certain she had.

He poked in a number, then hit the call button, and they both sat there as if waiting for another mobile to ring. But there was no sound.

Ivy felt as if she was holding her breath. That was likely because she was, in fact, holding it.

"I think we both know that I don't have any pockets," Giaco said after his factory-set voicemail message could be heard in the tinny distance of her mobile. He waved lazily at his bare torso and his boxers, and Ivy did her best not to stare at the ridges in that absurdly perfect abdomen of his, golden and gorgeous. "But as we can both hear, it certainly rang somewhere in this castle. Assuming I left the ringer on."

She had the strangest urge to ask him about his phone habits, and why he left his mobile lying about when surely he must have acolytes forever trailing around behind him in search of intimacies, but that all seemed… like the sort of conversation a person would have with someone they actually wanted to get to know.

Ivy already knew all she needed to about Giaco Tavian.

"Fantastic," she managed to say in place of any pointless questions. And she did feel that her throat was a little too dry for this moment of pure business and self-interest—on both sides, as far she could tell. Maybe it was that her tongue wasn't working the way it should.

She did not care to examine why that was. "I'll text you my email. I'll look forward to your response."

But Giaco didn't hand her back her mobile. Instead, he swiped through to something else and when she frowned at him, he leaned in closer.

As he no doubt meant it to do, his suddenly being *right there* got her attention. Completely. Ivy almost flinched away from him, but that would be telling and she did not wish to *tell* him anything she didn't have to. It took everything she had to stay still as he came closer, and then closer still. He lifted his head from his hand and let that hand move in a dreamy sort of arc until he was... touching her.

Not a brush of hands this time. Giaco was actually *touching* her.

She froze the way she had at that window. And this time there was no pretending she couldn't feel that inside, she burned bright.

He traced the outer edge of her ear with a fingertip and then slid his hand to hold the nape of her neck in his palm. She felt her lips part of their own accord, which she was sure she would be horrified by later, but she couldn't seem to do anything about it now.

Giaco leaned closer still. And then she heard the shutter sound of the camera on her mobile, a sound she often wondered if the youths these days even recognized. Since it had no relation to any machine they were familiar with.

But a random thought like that was her trying to put distance between herself and Giaco when there was precious little of it physically.

She should object. She should leap away. It wasn't as if he was holding her still. *She* was the one doing that.

But on the other hand, she felt as if she was wrapped up in that hand of his exactly the same way she'd imagined earlier. She couldn't breathe. His hand on her nape seemed to be directly connected to parts of her body she'd never spent any time thinking about too much, aside from their basic functions.

Ivy knew how to dress for her figure, but she couldn't think of the last time—or any time—that she'd ever felt the curves of her own breasts as if they were plugged in to some kind of wildfire current. She didn't understand how the faintest motion of his fingers against the tender skin beneath her ponytail could seem to flow down from that single point of contact to pool between her legs. Just as she didn't understand how she could feel golden and molten at once. Or how she could find herself captured completely by the look in his eyes.

Eyes that were much closer to her now. *All of him* was closer than he'd ever been to her before.

His gaze dropped to her mouth and seemed to hold there. And all of that molten gold inside her seemed to spin into something hotter, thicker—

But all Giaco did was sit back. Then he looked away, though he didn't move his hand, and she had to work not to give in to that trembling sensation she could feel deep inside her as he flipped through the photos that he'd taken. He looked back at her, and tossed the mobile onto the cushion between them.

"It looks like chemistry to me," he said. "Thank goodness. I hope you're ready for your tabloid debut, little saint."

Then, while she was still more or less gaping at him, he rose from his lounging position—taking that hand of his with him—and wandered back out of his father's office without so much as a backward glance.

Leaving Ivy behind to try to find her breath again—and pick up the pieces of her she hadn't even known could break apart like that, into all of that *golden heat*.

Then try to piece them back together as well as she could now that she knew that Giaco Tavian wasn't a joke. He wasn't a tabloid construction. He was *exactly* as lethally sensual as he appeared in every story ever written about him.

And Ivy was going to have to figure out how to handle him if she wanted her inheritance, like it or not.

CHAPTER FOUR

Two weeks later, Ivy was back in London, happily immersed in the life she'd built, and convinced that she'd allowed the simple fact that she'd been back in that castle to mess with her perceptions. To make her imagine things that weren't there.

Because she didn't like any other explanation for what had happened with Giaco. What she had *felt* while it happened.

In the first couple of days after all that—fleeing Italy as soon as she could make herself get up from that couch and managing to get home the same afternoon she'd left—she had jumped every time her phone indicated there was a new message. But as the days passed, she thought her nervous system was actually settling back into place. The more time elapsed between that day and now, the better she was. The stronger she felt.

The less delusional she was about what was or wasn't lurking behind the mask Giaco Tavian clearly preferred to wear. The simple answer was that it didn't matter. Her job was to sell a story to the outside world to get her hands on what her mother had left her, not to start an excavation project into a man who exulted daily in his supposedly charming disinterest in anything but the pursuit of his own pleasure.

She could get her head around work. *Work* made sense. Work was what had saved her when she'd come stumbling back to London, twenty years old with no skills and a sporadic education. Work was the lifeline she'd found to get her out of Umberto's castle of sick games and gaslighting that she'd been trapped in for too long. She'd found herself as she'd clung to it.

Why should this be any different?

Ivy thought the bracing British rain helped, too. Nothing like walking down London streets while it was bucketing down rain to make her forget all about *molten gold* or anything else remotely warming.

By the end of those two weeks, she'd decided that she'd embellished that morning in the castle. It had been nothing special. Just the Tavians up to their usual tricks, but she'd been in and out quickly and while she didn't have her inheritance yet, well. There was a path toward getting it. That mattered.

All the rest was just…the usual nonsense that could be chalked up to life in that family, in that place, in that desperate world that Umberto liked to marinate in.

She had better things to do than to focus on that kind of billionaire black-box theater.

When her phone buzzed one night as she was settling into bed after smiling so much during a fundraising event that her cheeks still hurt, she didn't react. She didn't even race to pick it up. She debated looking at her screen at all. And when she finally reached out for her mobile, she froze when she saw that the text was from him.

Tomorrow night, Giaco had texted. Rome.

She stared at that text for a good two minutes and while she did, she took stock of all the reactions she was having—none of which she liked. The elevated heart rate. The sudden flash of heat to accompany it. The fact that she was holding her breath. Again.

Ivy blew it out and ordered herself to *breathe*, for God's sake. I'm going to need more information than that.

And she realized that she expected him to flirt with her in text, or make some of his suggestive comments at the very least, when he didn't. Be at the airfield at 11 a.m. Don't worry about wardrobe.

She frowned down at that message for some time, trying to tease out all the variables. She wanted to ask him what he meant. Did *he* intend to dress her?

Ivy had to get very stern with herself when certain images flew at her then. She wasn't sure she wished to have a man sort out her wardrobe. Especially not when the entire conceit of what they were doing was that she was some everyday version of normal next to him.

Then again, she also knew that Giaco Tavian liked to play games.

Against her will, she swiped over to her photo app and pulled up the pictures he'd taken that day in the castle. She'd been so *unsettled*—that was definitely the right word, she assured herself—by what happened, by his fingers against her skin, that she hadn't even thought to look at them until she was on the plane and in the air on her way back to England.

Once she looked, she'd wished she hadn't. She'd felt as if her stomach dropped down out of her body and plummeted some 35,000 feet to slam itself into the Alps.

Because if she hadn't been fully present in the moments

he'd captured on her camera as they were happening—if she hadn't literally been there herself—there was no way Ivy would ever have believed that the people involved weren't engaged in an affair.

An *extremely carnal* affair at that.

Ivy didn't understand how he'd done it. There were three pictures and each one of them told its own story. In one, he was staring hungrily at her mouth while she looked utterly blissed out, her lips parted as if they had already kissed. In another, he was smiling at her—that twist in his lips—but this time there was no smirk in it. It was sex. It was *hunger*.

The final one was the worst. She didn't remember him moving back in to get closer to her, but it looked as if he was scant seconds away from pulling her onto his lap when she knew he hadn't been doing anything like that. Ivy-in-the-photograph looked as if she was on another planet, and he was its only sun, and she couldn't really parse how she felt about that. But Giaco…

Giaco looked *consumed* by her. His own lips were parted, as if he was breathing heavily, and it looked as if he was only inches away from taking her mouth with his.

She had deleted them all immediately.

But they had stayed in the recently deleted file, so since she was looking at them again—and not for the first time since she'd landed on British soil—she moved them back out. She told herself that it was forensic evidence, nothing more. It was a learning guide.

It was the way she was going to teach herself how to do what needed to be done.

Though it seemed that the answer was to simply let Giaco take the lead, no matter what it did to her nervous system. What these pictures taught her was that it didn't matter what she *felt*. It mattered how *he* made it *look*.

A thought that made her think about the discoveries she'd made in the castle that day. The ones that led her to be certain that his whole act was one big charade. Because if he could make things look anyway he wanted them to look, what did that say about all those splashy tabloid exposés that everyone took as the truth of him?

What was he hiding, she wondered, that he would do it in such a blinding spotlight?

"You will not get your inheritance or help a single orphan if you focus on the mysteries of one of the richest and most spoiled men alive in the world," she muttered at herself and set her mobile aside again.

But since Giaco was so good at these games and clearly loved to play them at all times, Ivy decided that the better part of valor was to not respond to his text at all. Let *him* wonder about something for change.

Assuming he ever did something so pedestrian as *wonder*.

The next day, she presented herself at the same airfield outside London where she'd caught Umberto's plane two weeks before. And once again, she was greeted by exquisitely polite staff who ushered her on board. She refused the offers of food and drink and told herself it was because she was preparing herself for whatever battles awaited her.

It was more truthful, if silly, to admit that there was some part of her that worried if she ate and drank something Giaco provided for her—however indirectly—she would be dragged straight down the rabbit hole and actually turn into that girl she'd seen in the photos he'd taken.

That girl she still had trouble believing was her.

Once in bright, sunbaked Rome, a waiting car whisked her into the ancient city and brought her to what she at first thought was a hotel, then realized it was a private house in a tony neighborhood, not far from one of the most famous squares in Italy.

She supposed it stood to reason that Giaco would live in a place like this, an eternal disaster in the eternal city, surrounded by untold centuries of the remains of creatures who looked just like him. Perhaps he was his own pantheon here, she thought as the car slid into a private courtyard that somehow managed to make it seem as if they were not in a busy city at all.

She climbed out, not surprised to find a different set of staff waiting for her. Though she was slightly surprised to find them standing *just so*, as if posing with the blooming wisteria canopy overhead—

You are confusing his staff with him, she lectured herself. *Not everything is a photo opportunity.*

"*Bongiorno*, Signorina Amis," said one of the women waiting for her. She stepped aside, making it clear that the old, thick vine marked the entrance to the house. "If you will come with me."

Ivy nodded and followed, expecting to be led into yet another sterile museum of a house, created entirely for clout and having nothing to do with the way that anyone actually lived.

This house was nothing like that.

It turned out that the beautiful wisteria was a hint that Giaco did not treat his house the way his father did. This house of his was eclectic. Surprising and interesting. The rooms were bright and filled with a haphazard sort of collection of things, from whimsical rugs to art that was clearly not there as investments, but because its owner liked it.

Or perhaps that was what he wanted her to think, she corrected herself.

It was not until they'd walked up a flight of stairs and into an open gallery that looked over a different court-yard below, this one green and lush with a water feature in the center, that Ivy realized this was actually a *home*. *His* home.

It was obvious, once she accepted the possibility that a person like Giaco Tavian could actually *have* a home that he poured this kind of energy into. There was no connecting or overarching theme between rooms. There was no *aesthetic*. If she had walked into this house with no knowledge of who might live here, she would have assumed that the owner was eccentric, had unlimited funds, cared deeply about comfort, and had a wicked sense of humor.

She wasn't sure which part of that shocked her more.

Her staff guide took her into a set of rooms that were clearly a guest suite. The woman looked askance at the small tote that was all Ivy had brought with her, but indicated that she should place it on one of the tables in the outer sitting room.

"The master has prepared a selection of items for you," she told Ivy. "The stylists will arrive at 3:00 p.m. But first, there are the looks, if you wish to take a peek."

She didn't wait for Ivy to respond, she simply walked into the next room, where Ivy found herself confronted by racks of clothing.

Ivy was no poor country mouse, overwhelmed by the sight of high fashion. By most standards, she lived a flash life. She went out of her way to appear to live even more bright and beautiful than she actually was. One thing she knew from her mother was that rich people loved nothing more than to give money to people who already had it. The more that Ivy presented herself as an *it girl* who happened to have a passion for charity, the more likely she was to get the donations she needed. Any hint of need or desperation and she'd get nothing.

She had a very nice wardrobe and she knew how to dress the part, but she was still surprised by everything that waited for her here. Outfits upon outfits, all of them extraordinarily beautiful—even the simplest pieces.

"This is much too much," she found herself saying, shaking her head. "I wouldn't even know where to begin to choose something."

"Oh, I'm so sorry," the woman said then, with a laugh. "He does not wish you to *choose* an outfit, Signorina. He has already chosen them all. There will be a series of encounters, you see. The master is very exacting when it comes to appearances and has created a *stylistic journey.*"

"A…stylistic journey?" Ivy echoed, sure she wasn't hearing any of this right.

The woman nodded enthusiastically. "You will start at this rack, and work your way through to the wedding attire."

Ivy decided she did not need to investigate *wedding attire* on this, the afternoon of their first, very fake date.

Her guide led Ivy over to the rack farthest to the left and pulled the first three items off. Ivy looked closer and she could see it was true. The racks were separated and color-coded, and this level of organization contradicted every single thing she had ever known about Giaco, to the point that she wasn't sure she could actually take it all on board. She cleared her throat.

"Forgive me," she said to the woman. "I can't believe that he actually put all this together."

"His assistant put it together," the woman said with another laugh. "Don't worry. You will meet Gabriele."

That wasn't a promise, Ivy discovered soon after. It was more of a threat.

Because when Gabriele swept in, he came with a cloud of stylists, barking out orders into one mobile while texting on another. He didn't knock. He simply stormed in and found Ivy in the sitting room, having succumbed to the lure of a meal since it was clear there was no avoiding the rabbit hole. She'd been answering emails, conducting her life as if she was back home and not tucked away in some ancient Roman town house, awaiting the pleasure of the man she had to pretend to marry.

"Everything about you is wrong," declared Gabriele in some mix of Italian and English, waving his hand in Ivy's direction. "*Meno male*, you're gorgeous!"

"Wait a minute," Ivy began, frowning at him. "There's nothing wrong—"

But Gabriele was already barking out orders to the stylists and Ivy couldn't help but be dragged along. Mostly because she suspected that if she didn't go along, she really would be dragged.

"There's a vision we are working toward," Gabriele told her as he hurried her out of the sitting room. "We have to highlight the contrast between you and il Padrone at this point. You understand."

"I don't," Ivy replied, which was hard to do when she was surrounded by what seemed like every stylist in Rome, all of them performing various beauty treatments on her. Whether she liked it or not.

There was a lot of waxing. Her nails were buffed, clipped, and polished—and her thoughts on color schemes were not solicited. She was hurried into the shower and then out. Her hair that she quite liked was subjected to a cut—*ever so little*, Gabriele assured her, *just to capture the shine*—and was then styled to look exactly the way it had before.

Except, she had to admit when she looked in the mirror, it was not *exactly* the same. There was something about it. The hint of a curl in her ponytail. The way it swooped, it somehow made her seem...

Something she couldn't put her finger on.

She didn't really get it until they dressed her in the outfit that had already been chosen for her for tonight. It was a pastel shift dress and a pair of darling shoes, everything not only her general size but seemingly created to her precise measurements. She didn't want to know how they'd managed that.

Or maybe it was more accurate to say she was afraid to ask.

Then, when it was all done, she got it. She stood before the mirror, hair and makeup and wardrobe done. She looked like herself, so there was that. But a different version of herself.

A very specific different version.

"I understand this now," she said, catching Gabriele's gaze as he stood behind her, texting furiously. "I might as well be Little Red Riding Hood setting off for the forest. And he'll be the Big Bad Wolf everyone already thinks he is, I suppose?"

"You understand this, *che delizioso*," Gabriele cried,

and he even grinned. "That's good. It's going to be a team effort, Signorina Riding Hood. This I promise."

Then she was once again swept away. Into the car, back onto the streets of Rome, and then back once more into a plane. This time it was an even shorter flight and when she landed, she found that she was in France. The Côte d'Azur, no less, and it was impossible not to be enchanted.

She was driven on roads that overlooked the gleaming, dancing sea, bright and blue. They drove from the private terminal in Nice along the coast until they turned right to drive into Cap Ferrat, ripe with villas and hushed elegance, and kept going until they pulled up to the Grand Hotel that had stood at the foot of the peninsula for some hundred years.

Ivy swallowed, hard. She knew this place. She had stayed here with her mother, in fact. There were pictures of her with both of her parents here, though she had only small flashes of her father in her memory, as he had died she was five. This hotel had always been about glamour. Any and every kind of glamour imaginable, as people with all kinds of power, from every corner of every industry, were drawn here.

But to Ivy, this was her childhood. The one she'd lost when her mother had packed her off to Umberto's castle.

"Il Padrone waits for you on the terrace," she was told, so she got out of the car and walked toward the iconic entrance of the hotel, feeling as if she was walking back through time.

She could see her mother in a convertible, Alana's hair swept back beneath a bright silk scarf, laughing into the sun. She remembered the parties, none of which she had been old enough to attend. Ivy had stayed hidden away in her hotel room, peering out the windows at the gleaming lights on the water, and the sound of clinking glasses and gaiety from below.

As she walked through the lobby, she nodded at the staff. Who greeted her by name, she noted, because that was the kind of place this was.

She made her way out back and found her way into a bar that opened up over the pools and the sweeping view of the Mediterranean Sea in all directions. And realized as she looked around that she wasn't looking for Giaco.

There was some part of her that was looking for her mother.

But it didn't make her feel sad. It felt more like a blessing. Ivy had almost forgotten that Italy and Umberto weren't the sum total of her mother's last years. She'd been happy here in France. She had loved coming to this part of the world, especially when the film industry gathered here, too. She had adored it when she could be among the people who understood her best because they lived the same sort of nomadic life she did, forever moving from one film set to the next.

Alana and Ivy had spent many a pleasant season right here, and yet Ivy had forgotten, somehow, that there was so much more to her mother's life than the way it had ended. And when she stopped looking for her mother, she looked out toward the gleaming sea instead and felt the truth of that lodge inside her too, like another benediction. There had been a whole, beautiful, sometimes heartbreaking life before Umberto. She'd been there for some of it.

I'm going to make more of an effort to remember you

happy, Ivy promised her mother then, in her head and her heart. *I promise.*

When she finally focused on the man standing by the rail, watching her with that same intensity that she couldn't believe no one else seemed to notice in him, she found she was filled with emotion.

That probably didn't bode well for this date of theirs, but Ivy couldn't regret it.

She gathered herself and walked toward him, noting that when Gabriele had spoken of a vision, he'd meant it. Giaco was dressed all in black. It was a flowing sort of black, a button-down shirt with the sleeves rolled up and loose trousers appropriate to the South of France. And yet somehow he gave the impression that he was both breathtakingly formal and charmingly informal at once. The shirt was open at the neck, showing off that gold skin of his. His hair was slicked back, but not like it had been when he'd come up out of that pool in Italy. This version gave the impression that he'd been running his hands through his hair all day.

Or, this being Giaco, someone else had been.

Ivy had expected to feel foolish, dressed up in a costume and made to look like someone who was playing the role of Ivy Amis rather than simply being herself. But as she walked toward him, that…wasn't how she felt at all.

For a few moments, it was as if everyone else on the terrace simply faded away. Ivy knew they were there but they were little more than shadows as she moved. It was the past that was brighter now. She heard her mother's laughter in her head, the most beautiful song imaginable and one she'd almost forgotten. She could see her father's smile, one of the few memories she had of him.

She could smell roses and lavender in this charmed place, but the only thing she could really focus on was Giaco.

On all of that dark jade, taking her in as if he'd been waiting all of his life for her to walk toward him, just like this.

She knew he was playing a role. But still, she could feel that look all over her. She could feel *him*. It was shocking to realize how good he was at this. If she didn't know better, he could have convinced her—easily—that he really was a man who had accidentally fallen in love and now had no idea what to do with it. And that he was something like a mess as he watched the agent of his destruction draw near.

He *looked* like he was made entirely of agony and hope and something far hotter, and she didn't know how not to be affected by that.

When she reached him at the railing, he turned toward her, looking as if he meant to grab her hand—

But didn't.

And that affected her too, because she could *feel* that near-touch like heat between them.

It occurred to her then that this was going to be significantly harder than she'd anticipated. For a number of reasons she hadn't thought to prepare herself to face. It was clear to her now that this was very likely going to make a mess of her, too.

And that was before she saw the pictures splashed all over the world the next day.

CHAPTER FIVE

GIACO THOUGHT IT was all going as well as could be expected. Better than that, even.

His relationship with Ivy Amis, who the papers were already calling *Saint Ivy* thanks to the excellence of his sales pitch and most tabloids' desire to stay in his favor, was splashed across every possible tabloid, in paper, online, on television, and on radio, too. The speculation was at a fever pitch and only grew as the days passed, staying forever at a boil.

He was excessively good at remaining at that same simmer, day in and day out.

Their first date in Cap Ferrat had caused an orgy of speculation. They'd appeared two other times that same weekend in various places along the coast, once the next morning on a stroll along the Plage du Midi in Cannes before disappearing into a café that did not allow paparazzi. The second, Sunday afternoon, while coming in from a yachting adventure.

That the virtuous daughter of the lost and widely lamented Alana Amis had spent the weekend with the Prince of Debauchery himself, her former stepbrother, had been talked about everywhere.

They had been seen in various places all over Europe

since. There were always just enough pictures to suggest a narrative without any posed photo shoots that would indicate it was all a deliberate stunt. This was one of Giaco's specialties.

A trip to Paris to take in the museums and stroll the boulevards, the way a pair of new lovers might. A dinner in Rome, hidden away in the back of a humble local trattoria, sitting close together and talking intensely, the way a new couple would do.

The two of them were caught exiting the car together outside a charity event in London, and then firsthand accounts about their behavior leaked out from within, with universal descriptions of Giaco's adoring behavior.

He had learned long ago that it was always better to create the story he wished the papers to run. And also that less was always more. The more it seemed that he attempted to keep his private life private, the more real people believed the things they saw were stenographers' renditions of his actual life.

Something he found he needed to remind himself of, lest he become too caught up in his own performance.

He pushed back from the table in his courtyard in Rome now and stood up, shoving his hair back out of his face. Ivy was still asleep in her guest suite upstairs— or he assumed she was still asleep, as she had not yet emerged—and the real trouble was that he was finding it increasingly impossible to ignore the fact that he was attracted to her.

At first he'd thought it was simply because she was beautiful. Who was he to swim against the tide of a beautiful woman? He'd never failed to appreciate beauty when he saw it before. There was no reason to start now.

But as the weeks passed, it had become terribly clear that this was something far more personal than a reasonable appreciation of feminine pulchritude.

The thing he had to keep reminding himself was that Giaco Tavian did not do *personal*. He couldn't afford it. He hadn't come this far only to toss it all away on a pair of blue eyes.

No matter how they seemed to see deep into the heart he could have sworn he didn't have.

He found himself staring up in the direction of her room, like a lovesick fool, and he hated that. It told him things about himself he refused to take on board. He turned on his heel and stormed through the house until he reached the pool he'd had installed on the lowest level, far away from any windows or prying eyes. He didn't bother looking for a swimsuit, simply stripping off his usual robe and boxer briefs and diving into the water.

It was crisp. A deliberate slap. He kept it cold enough to clear his head, but just in case the water temperature didn't do the trick, he started banging out laps. Down one length of the pool and back, over and over.

He told himself it was simply because he hadn't found any kind of release in far too long. He hadn't been kidding when he'd told Ivy that he required a significantly high amount of sex per day. He hadn't intended to forgo that pleasure, either, no matter what image he was projecting to the outside world. Despite what everyone believed—what he had worked so intently to *make certain* they believed—he was perfectly capable of discretion if it suited him.

And yet he hadn't done it.

He'd left the castle as soon as possible, putting the

necessary space between him and his loathsome father. Throughout the entire drive back to Rome he'd planned to call one of his trusted paramours as soon as he arrived. He had a very select few of them. They distinguished themselves by keeping their mouths shut and never imagining that there might be anything more between them than a hot, hard night in his sheets from time to time.

The less talking, the better. These particular women understood that when he called them, it was for a specific purpose.

But when he arrived home, he hadn't called anyone.

Later, when he and Gabriele had started discussing this particular media campaign, Giaco had decided that authenticity could only help push the narrative.

Besides, every paparazzo in Europe would go looking for proof that he hadn't reformed at all. They would dig into every connection he'd ever had—no matter how seemingly tenuous—looking for any indication that he was actually still the degenerate he'd always seemed to be.

And as discreet as he always was and as much as he had been able to trust his usual paramours for years, this was different. This was too important.

Giaco couldn't take the chance that any one of them might jump at the opportunity for a payday.

That was what he'd told himself. That was what he continued to tell himself as he grew hungrier by the day. And yet as he sliced through the water, all he could think about was Ivy. And not just that *appetite* inside him that he was determined to believe was simply because she was the woman nearest him—

But didn't. Not really. The craving was so intense. It didn't help matters that she was so intriguing.

He could not remember the last time he had been intrigued by anything or anyone. Giaco had always had a singular focus for the whole of his life, and everything else that came along was a casualty because of it.

But now, suddenly, there was Ivy.

And despite a lifetime of paying no attention to anything but his end goal and bonding with nothing but his own thirst for vengeance, he found that his fake girlfriend was actually fascinating.

I would love to be a sculptor, she had told him as they walked through the gardens at the Musée Rodin in Paris.

I didn't know you were artistic, he had replied.

It had been a great day, meaning it had been perfect for their purposes. They had walked about a selection of museums. They'd stayed next to each other, clearly together, and the pictures that had come from that day supported it. They'd looked lost in conversation, as if they might at any moment have reached out for each other, though it had been chilly.

I'm not at all artistic, Ivy had replied. *I know that there are those who believe that everyone has a certain amount of creativity lurking around inside of them, but I'm pretty sure that I missed that boat entirely. That's all right. In this life, I get to admire the creativity of others. And imagine what it must take to mold clay into such wonder with my hands, or find these perfect shapes in a block of stone.* She had smiled when she looked at him and only then had seemed to remember who they were. He'd found that he didn't much care for that, though he had opted not to ask himself why that was. *What about you? Do you have secret creative outlets?*

There's the obvious answer, he had said, almost by rote. She had actually rolled her eyes, which he'd found nothing short of astonishing. He couldn't remember the last time someone had dared. Whatever people might think of him, they had always taken him seriously in person. He'd assumed that was part of his so-called boundless charm. *And I assure you, of course, that my creativity in the bedroom knows no bounds.*

Of course, she said, still rolling her eyes. *The maestro himself, etcetera.*

Just so. He had gazed up at the statue before them, noting the exquisite lines and the emotion that seemed to be captured in hard stone, and could not have said why it felt to him like another impertinence. Maybe that was why he'd offered up something different. Something more than his usual playboy prattle. *I did paint once.*

Really? Ivy had shifted closer to him. Her head had canted slightly to the side as she'd studied his face. *Let me guess. You astonished everyone immediately with your innate and unstudied talent and could easily have been the next Picasso, had you managed to stop all the carrying on in the bedchambers of Europe? That sounds like you.*

I was appalling, he'd replied, and had then…actually found himself laughing. *Embarrassing, really. I would have been better off simply pouring the paints onto the canvas and spreading them about with my hands. I could have claimed that was modern art, at the least. Alas, it was a figure-drawing class and the goal was an adequate representation of said figure.*

He could still remember, pounding through the water in his cold pool, the way Ivy had laughed at that. As if he had surprised her. She had laughed so hard that she'd actually leaned against him, just for moment, as if his confession was some kind of connection.

The trouble with Ivy was that she made him feel like a regular man.

Giaco knew he couldn't have that. He couldn't allow it.

It would ruin everything.

He kept swimming until his arms felt numb, though it was a pity the rest of him refused to follow suit.

A few nights later, Giaco was convinced he had his wits about him again. A precious commodity, no doubt. Particularly when one was widely held to be missing a full set.

He had his people drop them at one of Rome's most exquisite and currently sought-after restaurants, currently vying for its second Michelin star. They were greeted at the door and then ushered to a table that was set away from the main dining room, as if—despite having managed a pap walk outside one of the hottest restaurants in the world just now—Giaco and Ivy were trying their best to stay private.

"You take your charity work very seriously," he said, realizing as he broke the silence between them that he sounded…awkward. When he was Giaco Tavian, who had never encountered an awkward moment his entire life.

This woman made him feel like some kind of untrained adolescent. The kind of adolescent he had never been, that was for certain.

Ivy looked at him, her blue eyes as fierce and piercing as ever. He always had the feeling she was as good as punching him straight to the chest. Every time she gazed in his direction. What he couldn't decide was whether she was doing something deliberately or if he was simply…*feeling* it like a blow.

When he had sworn off *feeling* long ago.

"Is this going to turn into one of your routines on my supposed canonization?" she asked coolly.

"Little saint," he found himself murmuring, "it's never *routine*. I am an endless font of new experiences."

"Not according to the tabloids," she retorted, a touch too quickly for his peace of mind. "They're quite certain you're up to your old tricks."

"The only old tricks they are ever referring to involve sex," he said, because he liked saying things like that in public places.

Even though it was unlikely that anyone could possibly overhear them, she always reacted. Though he could have used a far less socially acceptable word, he could still see splashes of color on her cheeks and the hint of it on her neck. Tonight he could see even more than usual because her hair was twisted up and out of her way, in another one of the seemingly casual yet elegant styles she wore now because they photographed so beautifully.

But her beauty wasn't the point here. What he could not understand was how Ivy had grown up in the same castle that he had and had somehow emerged capable of shame or embarrassment of any kind.

"I do take my charity work seriously," she said after a moment, her eyes a darker shade of blue. Clearly jumping right over the sex of it all, as usual. "When I moved back to London, I went with some friends to a charity event one evening and happened to hear a young orphan speak. She made me cry."

"You mean following your mother's funeral." Again, her blue eyes were on him. This time he felt certain that there was something like reproach in them. "You must have been very young."

Unbidden, the image of Ivy all in black, with only the searing blue of her gaze—shining bright with unshed tears as she'd stared down Umberto—came back to him.

Young, yes. But stunning all the same, though in his memory, it was now less because of the simple fact of her beauty and more about the deep fury she'd clearly been holding inside her.

It made the previous memory of her in the gallery doorway even hotter in retrospect, and if he recalled correctly, she'd been who he'd thought of anyway. His dirty little release.

"I'm still very young by any reasonable measure," she replied, with a laugh. "I suspect you and I only feel old because every day in your father's presence is like a decade. A long, grim decade." She reached out and picked up her wineglass. "And, of course, you actually *are* old."

That was so surprising that he laughed. "Apparently even the most holy martyr among us has claws when she needs them. Who could have imagined it?"

He thought she looked rather pleased with herself when she kept going. "My father died in a car accident when I was quite young."

"I remember," Giaco said. And when she looked surprised at that, he moved his shoulder in a shrug that did not feel like his usual elaborate, affected fare. Neither did his voice as he continued. "I was a teenage boy.

There were very few humans alive I admired more than Llewellyn Amis, the greatest action hero of all time."

The way Ivy smiled at him then made him almost feel as if he'd downed the entire bottle of wine himself. It was that bright, that warm. That dizzying.

"He always felt James Bond took up too much oxygen," she told him, leaning in closer to him, which did not help the dizziness any. "That's what my mother always told me. I don't remember much about him myself, I'm sorry to say. I knew my mother much better, and for longer. And I know all the stories she told about him. By heart."

She seemed to remember herself then, because she sat back. Or maybe, like Giaco, she was having trouble remembering the boundaries here, the lines between a good act and an actual conversation. Much less a real moment.

He had to swallow then, though his throat felt unduly rough.

Ivy cleared her throat. "In any case, there I was, all of twenty years old at a fancy charity do and I related so much to an orphan girl half my age that I really did cry. It's disorienting enough to lose one parent." She shook her head. "But you must know this yourself."

She gazed back at him then and he realized she expected him to say something about his own mother. His fierce, beautiful, highly educated mother had been raised by parents who had escaped from their homeland and had raised her to consider the France she'd been born in a foreign country that could never truly accept her.

He understood how she had seen Umberto as an escape from too many wounds that could never close. But she'd made a terrible mistake. And she'd known it.

"My mother chose her exit," he told Ivy, gruffly.

Though he didn't realize that he was going to tell her that until it was out of his mouth. He didn't understand himself. He never told anyone that. It was a secret— sometimes he thought it was a secret only he knew, as he suspected that his father had done what he always did and wiped clean any memories that didn't serve him.

Giaco expected Ivy to flinch or gasp in shock or make some other huge sort of movement that he could focus on and use to change course, but all she did was gaze back at him. Her fathomless blue eyes filled with what looked like…empathy.

God help him.

He ordered himself to stop, but instead he found his mouth opening against his will. "If you knew her, this would not surprise you in the least. She had always vowed that she would be no prisoner and when she determined that she had somehow ended up held in a situation she couldn't escape, she did what she felt she had to do."

No matter that it meant leaving a teenager and a six-year-old behind.

"I'm sorry," Ivy said after a moment. "That can't have been easy."

"I don't view it as a weakness on her part," he found himself telling her, stiffly. This was something he believed, deeply. Though it had never changed the fact of being left behind, it was a kind of comfort in its own way. "I am aware that my father likes to go on about her mental illness, but I always saw it as an act of extreme clarity. She knew exactly what she was doing. She left all of her affairs in order. She made certain to do it where she would be found by strangers and while that cannot have been good for them, I believe she was attempting to spare…"

"You," Ivy finished softly, when he didn't. When it seemed he couldn't. "She wanted to spare *you*."

And something about the way she said that seemed to grab him by the throat. Or maybe it was simply because he didn't talk about this, not to anyone, because everybody thought they already knew what had happened. It had been a major news story in its time.

Though that was all it was, Giaco knew. A story.

And the story was simple, if sad. Umberto Tavian's high-strung wife, after a long struggle with an incapacitating yet never defined mental illness, had locked herself away in a Paris hotel room and taken entirely too many pills. Deliberately. She had been discovered several days later, when housekeeping had entered the room despite the do-not-disturb sign after she had missed a raft of calls.

That was the story, though Giaco preferred his take. That it had been an act of defiance from a woman who had felt she had no other cards to play or places to go.

"I was sixteen," Giaco told Ivy. "Enough of a man by then, particularly in my father's house. I did not need to be spared though I do realize, in the fullness of time, that it was a gift she gave me." He shook his head. "I don't know why we're talking about this."

She smiled, though it was not a practiced thing. It was soft. Real, he thought.

"Orphans," she said quietly. "It inevitably leads to dead parents, I'm afraid." She reached over and put her hand on his forearm, if only briefly. "I'm sorry."

And he found he missed that touch when she took her hand back. Far more than was wise.

He sat back as their first course of food was delivered then, and he studied her as she interacted with the server. He marveled at how easily she had taken to this role she played now, when he knew it couldn't possibly be something she was comfortable with. She had never claimed to have her mother's ability to *inhabit* every space she occupied, simply by being *herself*.

Ivy was also glowing, which was a version of that, he supposed.

Having left nothing to chance, not for years now, Giaco had made certain that Ivy had every available stylist on call. Not to make her over, as she was beautiful without any help, but to carefully tailor her appearance so that over time, she looked as if she was on some kind of dimmer switch. Brighter and brighter in his presence, so that the papers would call it *love*.

Tonight she seemed brighter than should have been possible from a simple application of cosmetics, but something in him reacted a little too strongly to that notion. Maybe he wanted to believe—too much—that it was something else. Something more.

The trouble with all of this is that he was far too interested in this woman when he had only ever conceived of her as a means to his own ends.

And he couldn't lose sight of what was important now, no matter how she might *glow*.

Or how his forearm felt branded by her touch, well into the evening.

He lectured himself on these things all the way through dinner and then afterward, it all promptly went to hell when he took her hand as they exited the restaurant. "I thought we would walk back home," he told her, his voice gone gruff again.

And he could feel her immediate reaction to what he said. Not the walking part. *Home.*

Her reaction meant that he reacted, too. And it felt like a spark causing a flame and then a flame developing into fire in the space of a heartbeat. Or maybe it was simply that her fingers were in his, linked together, and he already knew that touching her was dangerous.

Giaco had always loved women. He was fully aware that his reputation suggested quite the opposite and he hadn't done much to fight that, but the truth was that he reveled in the female form. If he was an artist, it was in this. He delighted in the mysteries of a woman's body.

It would not have said he had a *type.* There was not any particular form or color hair or height that drew him in. He had been lucky enough to sample everything. And he had never regretted it.

But Ivy was something else altogether.

He spent significantly more time than he would ever wish to admit torturing himself with what else might have happened on that couch in his father's office, had he simply…followed the cues that he could read all over her body. Had he closed that last bit of space between them and set his mouth to the crook of her neck, the curve of her lips—

Giaco couldn't count the number of times he'd had to take himself in hand since that day, hoping to dispel this hold she had on him—but it always seemed to make the memory more intense.

She made the memory more intense. She made everything intense, when he had always prided himself on keeping everything *easy*. Simple.

Now they walked down the streets in Rome, melting into the crowds in this busy part of the only city he had ever truly loved, and he was *on fire*.

When all she was doing was holding his hand.

He could not for the life of him understand why such a simple, prosaic touch should hum through him like a thousand hymns sung in Saint Peter's Basilica, like this was something sacred.

It was nothing of the kind, of course. It was business and could never be anything else.

Giaco kept telling himself that.

When he got to a certain bit of shadowed alley that snaked between a few buildings and was set back from the street, he pulled her into the mouth of it with him, then backed her up against one stone wall. He propped himself above her, one forearm above her head, and looked down at her.

Though it was difficult to focus when her mouth was *right there*.

"You got the itinerary, I assume." He said it matter-of-factly.

She swallowed, and he watched the motion of her slender throat. "As you are no doubt aware, your assistant is nothing if not thorough."

"That is one of Gabriele's many strengths," he agreed.

"Yes," she said, sounding something like formal. She tilted her head back a bit more, and smiled up at him—though now she was back to the practiced smile of hers. He could not pretend to like it. "I read it. Did he write all that?"

"He did," Giaco said. And he could have left it there, because he already knew how little the whole world thought of his intellect. Most assumed he had none worth mentioning. But for some reason, he couldn't let Ivy think that. "He typed it up quite neatly as I dictated it, in fact."

"Then it's you, then," she said, and she was still looking up at him like that. As if they were standing in a shadowy place only steps from the crowd, bantering the way lovers might. Meaning, he knew, that she had absolutely read the itinerary. When he only stared down at her blankly, and only partly because he didn't know what she meant, she laughed. "I had no idea that deep beneath your indolent and cynical exterior beats the heart of a romance writer."

"I beg your pardon?"

"Because it's all so tidy, isn't it?" Somehow, her blue eyes seemed to burn even brighter here in the dark. "It's a perfect love story, delivered directly to the masses. Tonight our first kiss. Each outing will advance us into hints of more and more intimacy. This will inevitably lead to the perfect engagement with photos leaked to the press against our will, as if what we really want is to fly under the radar. And then, of course, we'll perform a spectacular wedding that makes our happy-ever-after a foregone conclusion. A triumph of three-act structure, Giaco. I had no idea you were such a dedicated story-teller."

"I am one of the greatest storytellers you will ever meet," he told her, not sure why his voice sounded so dark. "The best story I tell is me."

And he tried to make that come out like one of his

usual, drawling little barbs that made people around him think he meant the opposite of whatever it was he said. He tried to make it over into the usual sort of verbal performance art that he was so well known for, but it didn't work this time.

He could see it was perfectly clear to her, here in the hush of this alley while Rome swirled in all its bright noise and motion almost within reach, that it was nothing short of the stark truth.

"Giaco," she began.

"Pucker up, little saint," he ordered her, in that same dark voice. "It's time to be romantic."

And then he leaned in and took her mouth with his.

He felt her stiffen beneath him for just a moment, and then she kissed him back.

Giaco shifted and caught a glimpse of the paparazzo he'd explicitly tipped off tonight, lurking farther back in the alley. He knew all the best angles to use to give the man the proper photos. He knew how to kiss so that both he and his partner looked their best in the inevitable two-page spread.

But when she surged toward him, flattening her hands against his chest and arching into him, the kiss got deeper. Harder.

Not entirely within his control, though that should have been impossible.

He felt seized with some kind of fever. Or possibly that damned wine he'd had with dinner had gone to his head, suddenly and irrevocably. He felt as if he was spinning, and yet somehow there was nothing sickening about it.

There was only her.

Only Ivy, her mouth a bright, hot counterpoint to his

as if she was as swept away in this moment as he was. As he shouldn't have been.

His other hand found its way to her face, and wrapped around the nape of her neck, which he had spent too long now feeling like another brand in the palm of his hand.

This didn't exactly help. He cradled her head and he moved her where he wanted her to go. Because where he wanted to go was even deeper. Even wilder.

Even hotter, if that was possible.

And he could feel his whole body shudder into that blast of heat. He could *feel* her, everywhere.

He could smell a hint of the scent in the crook of her neck. It was something complicated, like citrus and cloves. Because, of course, Ivy Amis would never wear bog standard vanilla or anything else that smelled like sugar.

Giaco wanted to eat her alive. He thought maybe that was what he was doing.

He dropped his other arm from its lazy position propped up over her head and then he had both hands on her face, kissing her and kissing her. Her body was pressed to his and he could feel all of her, at last. Those plump breasts, pressed into him. The sweet, searing heat of her body, warming him.

His fingers were moving into her hair, threatening the pins that held it all in place, and the only thing he could think about was how best he could get inside her—right here in this alley—because he thought that if he didn't he might die.

She pulled away then, though that made no sense. Then she looked up at him, her chest moving too fast. Her blue eyes wide, and much darker now.

"Giaco…" she whispered. "We can't."

For a moment he had absolutely no idea what she was talking about. He couldn't understand why she would end something so perfect. So wildly *necessary*.

Then, like a key in a lock, it clicked. And he remembered himself.

Which is how he knew, in a rush of horror, that he'd forgotten himself in the first place.

He, Giaco Tavian, who had a preternatural ability to spot any possible hint of a camera from a mile away. He, who had set up this whole night and had literally written the script.

Giaco couldn't think of a single other time he had ever lost his head like that. He had never forgotten himself so completely. If she hadn't stopped him, he would have been deep inside her already—when he'd known going in that there was a paparazzo in this alley with them.

Because he'd called the man himself.

He pulled back and ran a hand down the side of her face, because he couldn't resist. Or he couldn't help himself. They were beginning to feel like the same thing.

There were no words, or possibly he couldn't speak. Instead, he took her hand again, led her out of the alley, and spent the rest of their walk home unsettled and something very much like thrown.

Because if he couldn't play this role of his in every possible circumstance, then the real truth was that Giaco didn't know who the hell he was.

And that had the power to ruin everything.

CHAPTER SIX

IVY WAS HAUNTED by that kiss.

However overwhelming she had found those pictures he'd taken of them and the scenes she'd imagined around them even though she knew none of that had occurred—well.

That was nothing next to the reality of the way he'd kissed her in that alleyway.

She'd been teasing him a little when she'd talked about his *romance writing*, because the truth was, she found the itinerary depressing. It wasn't that she didn't realize that a campaign like theirs had to be planned, it was the *extent* of the planning. It was dispiriting to have a script and to know at all times that they were following it. That those little glimpses that she got of him were probably not real. They were likely all part and parcel of the *intimacy code* that was on every entry in that itinerary on a scale from one to ten. The itinerary mapped out an emotional, intimate progression. Every time they were seen by the public, they should seem more connected, more into each other, more real.

And the more *real* they appeared, the more fake it all felt to Ivy.

Or it had, anyway. Until that kiss.

A kiss she had then seen hundreds of photographs of, splattered across every tabloid. A kiss that she'd relived again and again and again, every time she saw it.

A kiss that she couldn't help but think should have been only theirs—even though she knew that made no sense. There was no *only theirs*. There was only the performance they were putting on and the kiss was a major step forward with that—no matter how many snide reporters dismissed Ivy as but one more affair for a man who'd had legions of them before her.

No one believed they would last.

Ivy herself would not have believed it, except she knew exactly where they were headed and how long they'd stay there.

She had been surprised that he wanted to talk about her work with orphans at dinner that night. She had been even more surprised when he'd actually told her things about his mother. Much less what she was fairly certain was a huge secret, because she knew she'd never heard anything to suggest that the wife before Alana was anything but deeply unwell.

No one had ever indicated that her death was anything but a tragedy brought on by mental instability, and certainly not a clear-eyed, coolheaded, deliberate decision.

It had been weeks now and Ivy still found herself going over and over it in her head. The dinner. The way Giaco had actually *shared* with her. Then after. Back in London, she sat in the usual meetings and tried to look as if she was paying the kind of attention that she should have been. But she wasn't.

She kept going through that night. She felt like the silly sort of schoolgirl she'd never been, because she'd never had the experience of overwhelming crushes and packs of friends to giggle about those crushes with. Her mother had not liked to be left alone and so Ivy had been taught by a succession of tutors, none of whom had ever given her much of an education.

They'd been too busy wandering around starry-eyed in the castle, whether because they were bowled over by Alana's magic or sent into quivering joy at the sight of Umberto's riches.

Ivy had never thought that she was worse off for it. When she talked about her childhood and her schooling, she called it *eclectic*. And because she was lucky enough to not have to try to find the sort of employment that cared deeply about things like schools, she got away with it. It was seen as charming. It was never held against her.

So she had to hold it against herself as she found herself drifting off in the middle of a board meeting, paying absolutely no attention to the details of her own charity because all she could think about was the way their hands had fit together. As if they'd been separated cruelly from each other at birth and had only found each other again now. As if their hands had been *made* to clasp each other like that.

The way he tugged her with him into that alley and backed her up against the wall, so that all she could see of Rome, of the world, was the serious dark jade of his gaze.

Even thinking about that, about his *eyes*, made her whole body shiver into awareness. A rich, wild heat that seemed to consume her from deep between her legs, only to roll out so that there were flames everywhere.

And that was before she even got to the carnal magic of his mouth on hers.

In case she thought she was imagining all that, there were the pictures to prove it. Did she love them? Did she hate them? She could never decide.

The truth was he wasn't only affecting her job. He was affecting her sleep. Her breath. He was with her everywhere.

Just as the pictures of that kiss were everywhere. All over the papers. Impossible to miss online.

And she could admit—when she tried to turn off how she *felt* so that she could look at the pictures analytically, and with some kind of distance—that they were unquestionably romantic photographs. That must have been why they were getting attention even in places where she would have thought neither one of them was known enough to matter.

But it was hard to be analytical when she woke up on the nights she slept at all with her entire body on fire, his taste in her mouth, and the feel of his perfect, rock-hard chest beneath her hands.

Ivy just counted herself lucky that since no one believed that she and Giaco would last, she didn't have to worry about being hounded by packs of paparazzi the way he was. He and Gabriele had both assured her that wouldn't last.

She told herself to enjoy it while she could.

They continued to meet after the kiss, because that was what was in the bloody itinerary and the itinerary was the boss of them all. They attended a charity event in Luxembourg, a lovely opportunity to glitter and be seen while obviously head-over-heels. Intimacy code at six. They took a weekend away with each other, or so it seemed to the breathless public, in Venice to see an opera with much hand holding and *leaning*, intimacy still at six because it was public.

More pictures. More black-tie functions and society photographs. More indications that they were becoming a part of each other's worlds.

He didn't kiss her again. It wasn't on the itinerary.

And he only touched her when necessary, she thought. While dancing, for example. Or when ushering her with great solicitousness to a banquet table. Only in places where others could see them and marvel at the *taming* of Giaco Tavian.

Only when it benefited their little performance, that was.

One night she made a great show of scrolling through her mobile in the car, until he asked her what she was doing.

"Oh," she said, brightly. "I couldn't decide whether or not to put on lip gloss, so I was checking the itinerary to see if there might be more kissing. I wouldn't want to get that stickiness all over you, you understand. So tacky."

It was worth it, she thought, because of the dark look he threw her way. Then and when she spent the rest of the evening theatrically reapplying that sticky lip gloss.

Reminding them both about that kiss.

As if she was likely to forget it.

But their whirlwind romance was picking up speed and better yet, according to the excitable Gabriele, *inevitability*. Soon enough it was time to head off to a private island in the Mediterranean that was owned by one of Giaco's old friends. Or possibly Giaco himself—he had been offhandedly opaque about its provenance.

Ivy supposed it didn't matter, really. They weren't

going to interact with anyone. They were going to sell the big upgrade to their story—the impossible engagement of the world's most untamable lover to his personal saint—and deliver Umberto what he wanted. So that once they did, it would get them what *they* wanted. Win/win all around, or so she kept telling herself.

They took a private jet boat from Athens and were delivered to an unspoiled beach in the Ionian Sea. They were met there by staff who ushered them up steps carved into a rugged cliffside and into a gleaming villa that sat on top. A number of the staff members Ivy was used to from Rome came with them, and Gabriele was there too, because he would be directing this particular production.

While Ivy wandered around the villa, gazing out at the spectacular views of shining sea and white-sand beaches, rolling fields and lush olive trees, she could hear Gabriele in the background. He was barking out his orders, making sure that everything matched *the vision*.

When she heard a particularly frenzied bit of carrying on, she found her way outside to one of the terraces that looked out over the rest of the small island, making it clear that there was no one here but them. She found Giaco out there, standing at the railing much the way he had in Cap Ferrat.

"I'm sorry," she said. "I don't mean to intrude."

"I find it better to let Gabriele do his thing," Giaco said, without turning to look at her. "He will anyway, so it's better that he has the space to bring his various ideas to life. Otherwise we'll pay."

"It sounds as if some people are already paying," Ivy murmured. She moved to stand next to him at the rail, but not *too* close. They were both so careful in these un-scripted, uncoded, unplanned moments. If anything, it made her more aware of him, not less.

"He is invaluable," Giaco told. "I've never met another person who can so perfectly capture the public's imagi-nation. Gabriele is always on point. He always knows exactly how the scenes he stages will be received. It's quite a talent."

Ivy opened her mouth to ask him a question, but thought better of it. There was no need to ask, was there? Gabriele had been here long before she was. For years, one of the other staff members had told her. Since uni-versity, another had said. They had been inseparable ever since.

If it weren't for the fact that Gabriele had been mar-ried to his husband for the bulk of this time, Ivy might have been tempted to assume that all of the staging was to disguise Gabriele's relationship with Giaco himself. Before the kiss, that was.

The kiss had been clarifying in a multitude of ways.

Whatever it was that Giaco was hiding, it wasn't a love affair with Gabriele.

"What do you do when you're not plotting out these elaborate set pieces?" she asked now, her gaze on the sea in the distance.

"Haven't you heard?" Giaco asked her, and it took ev-erything she had not to turn and look at him. Because she was certain that she could feel all of that wild, dark jade beating into her. "All the world's a stage, little saint. I decided long ago that if that was the case, I might as well play out my part to my own satisfaction."

She did turn then. She couldn't help herself. "Is that how you'd describe yourself, Giaco? Satisfied?"

It was moments like this when she thought she saw so much...*more* there. That glittering dark gaze of his. The ghosts she was sure she could see move through his eyes. The way his face changed, as if he really was wearing a mask.

"I will be," he told her in a voice that matched his simmering gaze. "I can promise you that."

When he walked away, she felt as if he took part of her with him, though she couldn't have said what. Or why she found herself pressing her palm to her chest, right over her heart, as if that might get it back.

And a few days later she was back in gray and drizzly London, tucked up in her little house in Kensington, when all the pictures hit the media.

She knew they hit because her doorbell started ringing, loudly and repeatedly. It shocked her so much that she almost threw the door open to see if a neighbor needed medical assistance or perhaps a fire had broken out—but some shred of self-preservation intruded at the last moment. She paused and looked through the peephole instead.

And there they were. Paparazzi on her front door. Packs of them.

Because she was the woman who had finally claimed the eternal bachelor. She was the only one who had managed to do the thing no other woman had. She had the ring on her hand to prove it—and now the papers had the evidence.

Her time as a relatively private citizen was up.

Ivy backed away from the door and heard the old landline she'd forgotten about ringing. She didn't answer it. Instead she found herself running up the stairs to her bedroom, her heart pounding as if she was under attack, only to find her mobile under the same assault. So many messages. So many calls. But she was afraid to pick it up in case she accidentally answered the wrong person. The very idea made her feel panicky

She pulled out her laptop, ignored her inbox, and typed in her name at the top of her browser. And there they were.

Gabriele had put them through their paces. He had taken care of everything. It had been a beautiful day and had become a lovely evening—likely because Gabriele had decreed the weather needed to be perfect and it, too, had obeyed.

Staring down at the photographs, Ivy tried to make her memories match what she was looking at on her screen. She remembered walking down the path toward the cliff-top gazebo, the way lit by lanterns. Giaco had been waiting there for her. The photographs showed the two of them smiling at each other, sitting down, and enjoying a beautiful dinner overlooking the sea. In the pictures, she saw a couple lit up with each other. Consumed with each other.

And the truth was, she had felt that way while it was happening. But that was the thing about spending time with Giaco. She could feel whatever she liked, and she did, but no matter how sincere he seemed, no matter how intense it felt to her, she always knew that he was acting.

He sold it. There was no denying it.

All of the dinner pictures showed him entranced. Enchanted. He held her hand as they ate. He leaned in, as if every word that dripped from her lips was some nectar he wanted to taste.

And then, after their breathtakingly romantic dinner, were the money shots. The point of the whole thing. Giaco Tavian getting down on one knee and gazing up at Ivy, clearly proposing, a small jeweler's box in his palm.

She had to hand it to Gabriele, Ivy thought now. She didn't know if he'd summoned that breeze with the force of his will, but it made the flowing dress that she'd worn that night even more beautiful. The breeze caught it and played with it, and her hair blew back too, and it looked so intimate, so achingly romantic, that she felt something like teary as she stared at the photo now. At the look on Giaco's face as he gazed up at her. At the look on her own face as she put her hands on him.

She couldn't help thinking this was a scene that should never have been photographed.

In her house in London, with the phone still ringing and the doorbell sounding and hammering at her door, she sat back and rubbed her eyes.

"It isn't real," she reminded herself. Sternly. "None of that is real. No one is intruding on anything, because it didn't really happen."

They were engaged. That part was real enough. He had actually proposed, after a fashion, though what he'd actually said while down there one knee had not been romantic in the least.

Are you ready to take the next step? he'd asked. *It's probably going to make things difficult.*

Ivy had laughed. *More difficult than they already are?*

I've been with lot of women, he'd told her, as if she might have forgotten. As if anyone could possibly have forgotten. *The scrutiny on you will increase a hundred-fold.*

I'm aware of who you are, she'd replied, through a smile that had felt stiff on her mouth.

Then so be it, he'd said, rather darkly.

Not exactly love's young dream, Ivy thought now, but it certainly looked that way in the pictures. She looked down at her hand and felt that same jolting sort of reaction that she'd felt that night, too.

She'd had no doubt that Giaco would produce something beautiful. Every item of clothing that she'd been given to wear as part of her official wardrobe had been exquisite. She would be hard-pressed to think of a single objection she had to any of it. She even liked most of the pictures she'd seen of herself at these events. He'd staged romantic moments, took her to marvelous restaurants, and while their relationship might have been fake, the food was always divine. She'd assumed the *engagement upgrade*, as noted in the itinerary, would be the same sort of thing.

In terms of the ring Giaco would choose to sell their engagement to the world, she expected something extravagant, but elegant. Instead he'd gone sentimental, and she still didn't know how she felt about that. The ring was a collection of opals and moonstones, clustered around a diamond.

I love moonstones, she had whispered, out there in the soft breeze on a Mediterranean cliff top. *My mother loved opals.*

I know, Giaco had said, all dark jade and that mouth set to something near enough to stern. *You forget, Ivy. I did actually know your mother. And you.*

The photographer had kept snapping pictures from his perch on the roof that the public would confuse for a drone, and so she could see the exact moment she'd looked down at the ring, that intense look on her face. What it looked like to anyone who was seeing this photo now—and she assumed the world had seen it already— was that she'd been fighting back tears.

When what she'd actually been fighting back was a sense of disorientation. *No*, she had told him, the ring gleaming between them. *You don't know me. You certainly didn't know me back then.*

I know you like moonstones, Giaco had replied. A bit stiffly. As if she'd offended him.

She hadn't seen any reason to push at that assertion, even if she'd wanted to. Even if it had been like a burning thing in her throat, the need to correct him. Now, hidden in London these last few days in preparation for this photo drop, now with a baying mob outside her door, she huddled in her bed and stared at that ring on her hand.

The ring he'd put there when she'd stopped arguing about whether or not Giaco Tavian *knew her*.

It was, bar none, not only the most beautiful ring she'd ever seen, but it was also essentially what she would have designed for herself if she could have. And that made her feel…

Well. She didn't know what she felt. Not about the ring, anyway. Or maybe she didn't really *want* to know how she felt, because—

Her mobile rang again and she looked over out of habit, then picked up only because it was Giaco's number.

"I take it you've seen the pictures," he said without preamble.

"I think the entirety of the British gutter press is kept out of my doorstep." She laughed, though it came out a bit...wild. "They clued me in."

"I thought that might happen." He sounded odd, she thought. Or perhaps he *didn't* sound lazy and mocking and unbothered by it all. "We'll issue a statement from here. But this is what I meant by things getting difficult. I don't think this is the kind of furor that's going to die down, Ivy. You're too exposed in London."

"I wouldn't call myself *exposed*," she argued, though she certainly *felt* exposed. She kept looking over at the window as if she expected the mob to levitate up from the street. "There are any number of people in this neighborhood who command more attention than me—"

"That was yesterday," Giaco said curtly. "Now you are engaged to one of the most famous men in the world. You no longer live in the same world you did when you went to sleep last night. And the level of interest in you, particularly this kind of tabloid interest, will no doubt make your high-profile neighbors nervous, which I'm certain they'll make clear to you soon enough."

She wanted to argue with him. But her doorbell kept ringing and ringing and ringing. So did her landline. Ivy was beginning to feel a headache developing in her temples. She had the strangest sensation that a barrier had been crossed here. A boundary, maybe.

That there would be no going back from this, no matter what happened.

And she wasn't sure how she'd ever imagined that she wouldn't end up here. Still, she found it *surprising*. *Upsetting*. Or maybe she didn't really mean to use either one of those words. What she felt was...too much.

She wanted to cry. She wanted to run downstairs, fling open her door, and shout at everyone who was standing there, forming a scrum outside, possibly already rooting through her rubbish in the back. She wanted to rewind back to that meeting at Umberto's office, and tell him to go to hell.

She wanted to live forever in that kiss, which paradoxically enough still felt to her as if it was only theirs.

When it wasn't, of course. None of this was real. None of this was hers. None of this mattered outside of this production they were putting on.

The kiss that still haunted her had been published just like these pictures were. It was part of the body of work that they were giving the world so that everyone who wished could tear it apart. Dig into it. Make it theirs.

She would do well to remember that.

Just as she would do well to remember the orphans who were the reason she was subjecting herself to all this in the first place.

Ivy rubbed at her temples and then closed the screen of her laptop with a decisive click. She closed her eyes. "What do you suggest we do next?" she asked, and was proud of herself for sounding nothing at all but businesslike.

When she felt anything but.

His team descended upon her house within the hour, indicating to her that Giaco had anticipated this response. They cleared out the paparazzi and whisked Ivy away. She read the prepared statement from Giaco's representative—Gabriele, she assumed—who expressed horror and disgust at the violation of their privacy and the revolting response that had made his new fiancée feel as if she was under attack during what should have been a happy time in their lives.

It was a terrific statement, Ivy could see. Public sentiment swung hard toward Giaco and Ivy almost immediately, with commenters across all platforms decrying the intrusion and the publication of what was surely meant to be a completely private moment.

And that was how, with very little discussion, in the course of a few days she found herself not only engaged to Giaco Tavian but completely moved into his house in Rome.

Not into his bedroom, of course. That would be taking things too far. That would be *real*, and whatever else happened, she knew *that* wasn't allowed. *Maybe you should ask yourself why you're thinking so much about his bed*, a small voice inside her kept asking.

She found herself sitting in his pretty, private courtyard one evening, still not certain she was adjusted at all to this new life. She couldn't go to work. She could conduct video calls with her charity, but she didn't feel it was the same. She thought that every call seemed to get caught up somehow in all the questions these people she'd worked with for years didn't dare ask her directly.

Ivy grew tired of the courtyard, for all that it was pretty and soothing. She grew tired of staring at a water feature, wondering what else in her life was going to change. Wondering why she hadn't anticipated any of this when everyone else clearly had.

She walked back into the house, wondering why it was Giaco had known that she would end up here. Probably from before their first date, or he wouldn't have installed her itinerary-friendly wardrobe in her suite. She was tempted to think he'd planned all this.

But even as she thought that, she didn't think that was entirely fair. *Planning* suggested a whole different level of machinations. What he'd been—and what she had not been, clearly—was prepared.

She had to get a new mobile. Ivy had thought that she was used to a certain level of notoriety and celebrity, because she certainly traded off that in London. In all the circles she moved in, for that matter. Everybody knew who her parents had been.

This was something completely different. It was on a whole new level.

She understood in a brand-new way why Giaco lived the way he did. It only occurred to her now that he had chosen this house because it was built like a medieval fortress. The public could camp out at the outer entryway all they liked, but there was no access to the house itself. They couldn't peer in his windows or bang on his doors. Not to mention, she began to realize that half the staff that he employed here were, in fact, his security force.

Meaning he was not quite as lazy and feckless as he appeared.

She came upon him while she was still feeling out of sorts and glared when she found him lounging in one of his outrageously comfortable armchairs in what she was fairly certain was his library, though *he* called it a study. As if to distance himself from what it might say about him if he had an actual library.

Though the shelves upon shelves of books told a different story.

"Why didn't I know how difficult your life is?" she demanded.

Giaco did not look up from the book he was reading. She filed that away to come back to later. The fact that he was reading a book at all. The fact that the book he was reading looked big and thick and dense, and he appeared to be in the middle of it. Yet more evidence that he was not who he played in the press.

And in private much of the time.

"I'm delighted that someone has finally noticed the great burden that I bear," he said without looking up. "It is amazing how few seem to care about my many travails. But I'm telling you, Ivy, long have I struggled with all of this beauty and wit. It is a curse."

"I meant your lack of privacy," she snapped at him.

"That is a feature, not a bug," Giaco told her, finally lifting his gaze from his book. "I determined long ago that it was not fair to the world to conceal the glory that is me from the public. They have so little, do you not agree?"

Ivy did not agree. She stood there, staring at him. She took in the state of him, lounging here in the privacy of his own home yet still dressed as if he expected a photographer to happen by at any moment. One of those buttoned-up shirts of his that he never managed to button to the top. Those loose trousers made her think of islands in the sea. He liked his feet bare in the house, she noticed, and she wondered at the contrast between the outrageously debonair figure he could cut when he chose to, all black-tie sophistication and urbane grace. This was a far more casual version of him.

"None of this is real, is it?" she heard herself ask.

Something changed. She watched it move over his face and then his gaze was different, too. Almost…cannier, perhaps.

"Are you talking about our relationship?" he asked quietly. "The one that has currently captured the attention of the entire planet? No, my little saint. It is not real. Have you become confused?"

"I'm not talking about that, I'm talking about you," she said. "When I first saw this house I thought that it seemed so authentic. A real home that someone lived in. That someone is you, but you don't live anywhere, do you? You merely…exist between photo ops. Isn't that right?"

It was possible that she was being too harsh. But this was some strange amalgamation of all of these unwieldy feelings that she'd been combating since the start of this. Maybe it was the ring. Maybe it was that damned kiss. Maybe it was the fact that she felt as if she'd been hunted out of her own home, like a hapless fox.

Maybe it was just that she didn't like feeling hapless *or* hunted.

Also, she thought it was true.

"How astute," he said, in that cutting way of his.

He set his heavy book aside. And then he was rising up with more of that impossible effortlessness of his. All of that athletic grace. It set her teeth on edge.

It did more than that. It made her remember the taste of him, and the way that perfect, cruel mouth of his had coaxed so much sensation out of her. Perhaps he'd even licked it *into* her. It was too much.

He was too much.

"You're putting on an act so no one can see who you really are," she managed to say, though his gaze was trained on her now and he was heading her way. "Aren't you?"

"Thank you," he drawled, drawing closer. "Without this incisive psychiatric breakdown of my innermost self, how could I possibly go on?"

"Obviously everybody plays certain roles as they go about their lives," she said, frowning up at him as he came upon her. "But not the way you do. You literally have a director on staff. You have an entire production team. Do you think that's normal?"

She didn't realize that he'd backed her up across the whole study until she had to stop because there was something in her way. A glance behind her told her she was standing at the back of the sofa that faced the currently unlit fireplace.

But if he noticed that he'd pinned her, he certainly didn't seem to care.

"Everybody lies," Giaco said in that same quietly dark way. "If you don't think that someone is putting on a performance for you, you're not looking closely enough. Let's talk about your performances, shall we? Lady Bountiful. Saint Ivy of the Orphans, casting her goodness all about her like palm fronds. Who are you when you're at home, I wonder?"

"I suppose we'll never know," she retorted, "as I was chased out of my home by the demon horde you have on speed dial."

"What I cannot understand is this act," he replied, as if she hadn't spoken at all. "You were raised in celebrity. It has touched every aspect of your life. Yet you act as if no one ever told you that it was a game, and I cannot account for that. You're damn right that *I* play it, and well."

"Do you play it?" she asked, leaning closer to him. "Or at this point, is it just playing you?"

Giaco leaned in, his hands gripping the back of the sofa on either side of her body, caging her there. "I don't care," he murmured.

And then his mouth was on hers again.

It was as if sheer exultation was a tap that he could turn on and off, because it flooded her. And it occurred to her only now, only with his mouth on hers, only when she could arch forward and wrap her arms around his neck and press her body to his, that this was exactly what she wanted.

That maybe all those feelings she couldn't quite name were this.

A deep yearning for *this*. For him.

For the way his hands seemed to know her body so well, so easily. They moved over her, stirring up a restless hunger everywhere he touched her. One moved over her hair, caught back in a loose, messy braid. Another moved down her back, then tested the curve of her butt.

It had been a warm day in Rome and she was wearing a loose pair of shorts that she sometimes slept in, too. And a tiny little tank top because she'd been sitting out in the courtyard, encouraging the sun to dust her skin something more than its usual pale white.

Now she wondered about her motivations for that, too.

But the thing about Giaco was that he didn't seem to wonder about anything.

He just did as he pleased.

His hands moved to the low waist of her shorts and then his fingers slid beneath the elastic band, and then it was happening.

It was so smooth, so inevitable, that she didn't have time to process it. It wasn't happening and then it was—his long, hard fingers curving into her heat, slipping beneath her panties she wore and finding her molten hot folds.

He stroked her there, he stirred her up, and she hardly knew what to do with herself. Her hands were fists in that shirt of his, and he moved—shifting her up so she was straddling one of those thick, muscled thighs of his.

And still he played with her core, his fingers working a magic she hadn't understood as possible until this moment. All the while he kept that thigh a hard pressure between her legs, and she couldn't seem to help herself. She rocked against him, and his fingers didn't stop, and there was a rocking and the pressure and the friction and—

She shattered, hard and wild. It came fast and hot, like a punch. Then she shook and shook against him, her head falling forward against his chest.

Giaco muttered something she couldn't understand and then shifted her again, this time pushing a finger deep inside her.

Then it began all over again. The rocking. The heat. The inexhaustible build—

This time, when it hit her, she cried out.

And then stood there, bewildered, because he was suddenly…gone.

It took a terrible effort to come back into herself.

He wasn't *gone*, she realized. Giaco was standing a few feet away from her with a stark look on his face. She couldn't quite read him.

But she could see that enormous cock of his, pressed hard against the loose fabric of his trousers. She was still riding through her aftershocks and she couldn't imagine what she must look like to him, her mouth wet from his. Her whole body ravaged, and shaking. She wasn't even sure about the state of the shorts she was wearing, much less how far up her abdomen her tank top had rolled.

Yet Giaco looked at her as if she was a ghost.

Then he turned, abruptly, and left her there.

And it took her a long time to catch her breath. Ivy stood there, still gripping that sofa, until her heart settled down. Until her body calmed…

To some degree, anyway.

It was tempting to see what had happened as some kind of cruel rejection, but she didn't.

She thought about that kiss in the alleyway and how she'd been the one who'd had to break it. How she'd been the one who'd had to step back, and how she'd thought at the time that he'd looked a lot as if that wasn't something he'd been about to do at all.

And here, now, that *look* on his face.

Ivy had a deep certainty inside her, then. It wasn't something she would have wanted to defend, but she knew it was true all the same. She was pretty sure that Giaco had exposed himself tonight.

Because surely, if he was the cynical, emotionally detached fuck boy that he liked to pretend he was, he would have simply tossed her down on the couch behind her and been done with it. She had the strangest notion that what she'd seen tonight was his true face.

She had accused him of wearing a mask, and then he'd dropped it. If he hadn't, why would he have bothered to run away?

And later, when she stood in the shower in her suite,

she was even more certain of two things. First, that she was never going to sleep again, not with all of this in her head now. And second, that the more she saw of him—the more real parts of him he showed her, whether against his will or not—the more she wanted him.

Not because they were playing their parts.

But because she was starting to think that Giaco Tavian really was the narcotic everyone claimed he was, after all.

CHAPTER SEVEN

THE ORIGINAL PLAN, thanks to a timeline handed down by Umberto, had been to carry on with the romance over the summer. To tease it out to the public, particularly now that they were engaged, and continue stoking the flames of all the public's interest until it was nothing short of an inferno.

But after that night in Giaco's favorite room in his house in Rome—his personal library that he doubted he would ever enter again without remembering the little noises that Ivy made in the back of her throat right before she came—Giaco decided that the timeline needed to be accelerated.

He could have discussed this with everyone involved. He could have called a meeting, solicited opinions, and taken notes, but he didn't.

Instead, he allowed himself to be captured by a group of reporters as he was enjoying an excessively priced espresso in a famous café that sat not far from the Spanish Steps. Not a place anyone went for privacy.

"Don't you think that you and your stepsister are moving too fast?" one of the reporters shouted at him as he left the café and presented himself on the busy Via dei Condotti, bustling with foot traffic and thick with tourists.

Giaco laughed. "I don't," he told them.

Then he shrugged and made sure he looked *rueful*. Not a look they were used to seeing from him, so the pack of them quieted down immediately.

"I never expected to fall in love," he said simply. "But now that I have, I naturally wish to be with her. Always. I want forever, immediately." He smiled. "I'm still the same man I ever was, my friends. Instant gratification has always taken too long for me."

So it was that Umberto, who no doubt would have ordered him to stick to the original itinerary if he'd suggested any changes to it, called Giaco the very next day and demanded that the wedding be held as soon as possible.

The old man was entirely too predictable.

Giaco and Ivy were both at home that night and he opted not to dwell too much on how using that word—*home*—to mean the place where both of them lived… got to him. Because he didn't think that it should have. It should not matter to him at all. After all, she had her own set of rooms and they barely saw each other.

He made certain of that, in fact. Ever since that night in his study—

But he tried not to think about that.

Which was to say, he woke in the night, broken out in a full sweat and his cock so hard it hurt, wondering why the hell he'd walked away from her.

"We decided to accelerate the wedding timeline," he told her, in as dry a voice as possible. As if they both worked on a factory line somewhere and he was discussing something as arid and unemotional as the mechanics of the machines they used.

He'd come upon her on one of the laps she took around the open-air gallery that looked down on the courtyard. He knew her routine by now. She woke in the morning and had a light breakfast. Sometimes she visited the gym tucked away in the corner of his house. Other times, there was a certain thumping from her room that made him think that she did the sort of workout videos he knew were available everywhere now. She spent much of her day taking calls and sending emails. And then in the evenings, she liked to walk. They didn't walk out into the city unless it was planned out in advanced, so she did it here.

He stood in one corner and watched her as she moved. And he knew that she saw him and had heard him, but she didn't say anything until she came back around. She stopped then, a few feet away from him. "Why?" she asked. She studied him. "I thought the itinerary was an immutable document, inerrant and inflexible."

"You object?"

"I have no feelings on it one way or the other," she said, and Giaco felt extremely virtuous that he did not call her out on her emotions. Or the fact that she was lying. He could see it written all over her, though he kept that to himself. Besides, she kept going. "Obviously the sooner we're in, the sooner we're out, and that works for me. But since this is an enterprise that we're both engaged in, I think you should probably update me on what's really happening."

"Love," he said, because it turned out he couldn't help himself. Not really. Especially when she frowned. "Everyone loves a love story, my little saint. I think it might be best to strike while the iron is hot. And while so many people remain this deeply interested in us."

"You haven't told me why you're really doing this," she said then, surprising him. He decoded that he already regretted this interaction. Her skin was glowing from her walk in the sultry evening heat and he didn't need further reminders that she was, by far, the most irresistible woman he'd ever encountered. "It can't only be money."

"Whyever not? Isn't that why you're doing this?" He didn't wait for her to answer that. "We leave for the castle tomorrow. The wedding will be this weekend. It will seem the obvious conclusion to this glorious whirlwind we're caught up in. I can't wait to read all about it."

"Me neither," she said, that blue gaze of hers a little too intent on his. "After all, you can find the truth of things in the strangest places, can't you?"

He opted not to answer that, either.

Though being subjected to Ivy's entirely too all-seeing, all-knowing gaze seemed like a far better option than finding himself seated at an extremely awkward family dinner later that week.

It was the night before their hastily arranged wedding. Umberto had been complaining bitterly for days about the extremely powerful people whose schedules he'd had to ask them to rearrange in order to attend.

I suppose we'll find out how powerful you really are, Giaco had said with an excessively insolent shrug, lounging about bonelessly in his father's office. He'd been trying his best not to remember the last time he had been in his father's office, mesmerized by his former stepsister's shocking beauty. Proving to her that there was chemistry in the pictures he'd taken when he'd already known that there was chemistry. He'd felt it immediately.

It had taken an effort to concentrate on his father's sneering, profane response. He'd only shrugged again. *If you are as omnipresent as you believe, surely they will all drop everything to dance attendance upon you*, he'd said. *How clarifying it all will be.*

All you need to do, his father had growled at him, *is get married tomorrow and keep doing whatever it is you're doing to convince the world that you had a beautiful, virtuous change of heart. The love of a good woman and all that shit.* Buon lavoro, *and so on.*

Giaco had found himself having the entirely uncharacteristic urge to argue with his father. To tell him that, in fact, he would be lucky indeed if a woman like Ivy loved him. And he had been so appalled that the idea of saying such a thing to his father had even occurred to him that he was still recovering from it now.

His father had insisted that the family gather together. Giaco couldn't say he understood why. As far as he knew, Umberto was as disinterested in his children as he was, historically, in his wives.

His younger sister, Leontina, sat opposite Giaco, her posture perfect. She looked like a dancer, he thought. The sort of ballerina who had been caught in a music box, kept under a glass shell, never to see the light of day unless someone wound her up. In the castle, of course, no one ever did.

He had done his sister the very great favor of giving her his distance. He had taken the brunt of his father's temper as best he could, and he knew he was the child who most often drew Umberto's fire. He'd thought that was the best he could do for a younger sister he hardly knew.

Only tonight did it occur to him to wonder if perhaps he might have taken a different tack with her. Perhaps offered the family she hadn't otherwise had. After all, he was the one who had known their mother better. He'd had that gift.

Giaco did not share his musings with the group.

And not only because he didn't like how said musing made him feel about his actions as a brother all these years.

He turned his attention to his soon-to-be-bride instead, a surefire way to distract himself.

Ivy looked stunning, as always. Gabriele had thrown several epic fits about timeline readjustments and then had come through, as always. Ivy looked like a dream. Her blond hair was piled on top of her head and the moonstone and opal earrings she wore set off her ring beautifully. She was dressed in shades of cream, like a good bride-to-be.

Once again, he thought of the way she'd clenched around his finger and nearly embarrassed himself right there at the table.

The silence in the room marched on, unabated, as this was not a family who *chatted*. It was a dire, quiet meal, while everyone who wasn't Umberto waited for the inevitable explosion. Surely everyone else could feel it, pressing down on them like so much memory and too many ghosts.

It took Giaco all the way to the sullen dessert course to realize that normally, he would have provided the comic relief and/or the drama for the evening. He would have been outrageous from the moment he'd entered the room. He would have poked at everyone around the table, made withering remarks on the one hand and talked in overwrought innuendo on the other. He would have made everyone so uncomfortable and so furious that it was likely at least one person would have stormed off, and he would have laughed his way all through it.

That had been his primary role in this family for as long as he could remember. He poked. He prodded. Whatever thunderous, scathing thing his father might like to say or do, Giaco would ruin it in advance. He would steal all the thunder out of the room before it had a chance to start the faintest bit of rumbling.

And he knew why he did it, too.

But his mother would not thank him for continuing to pander to this man, even if it was only make-believed and peppered with a good deal of provocation, too. Not after she'd affected her own escape the moment she'd thought Giaco was old enough to do without her. Not after she'd decided that she no longer wished to worry about any pandering herself when what she could do instead was be done with it.

The trouble was that Giaco couldn't access that version of him any longer. He could picture that version of himself in his own mind. He could see the sorts of things that he would have said in a situation like this. It wasn't even hard. It was all right there, on the tip of his tongue.

Yet he also understood that it was what Umberto wanted. It was why he'd forced them all to sit down to this unpleasant dinner in the first place. He *wanted* reasons to shout, to be furious with his son. To have more reasons to threaten Giaco.

That Giaco was not giving it to him fit with Giaco's supposed acquiescence to his father's demands. It was all part of the plan. What had never occurred to Giaco, in all his plotting, was that *not* acting out, *not* indulging in a battle of wits with the father he found ill-equipped, would feel like amputating his own limbs.

Umberto probably wouldn't have minded if Leontina got mouthy instead. Or at least if she drew a bit of fire, as hard as that was to imagine. That would give Umberto an opportunity to berate her for the quiet, forever-hiding-in-plain-sight personality she'd cultivated to deal with him, because Umberto took pleasure in making the people around him feel small.

Giaco could see exactly how to start poking at everyone to make Umberto huff away again tonight, muttering threats at his only son as he went. He'd done it a thousand times before. He'd protected his sister this way. He'd even protected his mother, back in the day.

It was satisfying to draw fire from Umberto, because all Giaco did was laugh at the old man. Which, predictably, drove the narcissistic asshole up a wall.

But despite the fact that everything in him *wanted* to do it, and he felt somehow misshapen because he was playing the part of the dutiful son he wasn't, the real truth was that he didn't seem to have it in him anymore.

Giaco stared across the table at Ivy, whose fault this was. He might not know what was happening to him, not really. He wanted to say that it had started that night in his library, but he knew better. It had started before that.

It had started the moment he'd looked up from that damned hot pool to find her watching him from the window.

The supreme unfairness of this happening now, when

he could least afford a misstep, wasn't lost on him. He was just lucky that he'd intended this little show of meekness. That this wasn't throwing the whole plan into disarray.

"Well," Umberto said, glowering at the rest of them as he stood abruptly from his chair. "I don't know that I've ever had a meal more tedious. I expect all of you to be on exemplary behavior tomorrow. Or there will be consequences. *Dire* consequences."

Then he stormed from the room after all, no poking or prodding required.

Ivy blinked. "He does realize it's not his wedding, doesn't he?"

"It's all his," Leontina said then, looking up from her lap briefly. Her eyes widened as she looked from Ivy to Giaco. "You must have noticed already. It's his world. We live in it only because he allows us to."

"You don't actually believe that," Giaco said, frowning at his younger sister. His much younger sister who, as far as he knew, had always believed that their mother—who'd had Leontina as a last-ditch effort to fix her unfixable marriage, only she had not come out a boy—had not died on purpose.

He had made certain she'd never thought that. He'd gone out of his way to make sure she thought their mother hadn't had a choice about whether or not to leave her. It only seemed right.

"It doesn't matter what I believe," his little sister told him, her gaze grave. "It only matters what *he* believes. I don't think you've been paying attention."

And then she left the table, so that it was only Giaco and this woman he would marry the following day. This woman who he should never have turned around and seen through that window. This woman that he should never have touched.

She stared back at him for a moment that quickly became uncomfortable. Then she rose from her seat and made her way over to the windows. It was early summer in Tuscany now. The hills were covered in wildflowers. Everything was lush and green. Outside, the sun was still busying itself with setting and the sky was orange, melting into the dark hills and making them glow.

But he had long since ceased to find anything more beautiful than Ivy.

"Imagine when we'll be gone from this place again and that man won't matter anymore," she said quietly.

And that hit Giaco harder than it should have. Harder than expected, anyway. He would have said that there wasn't much that anyone could say about his family that would bother him any longer. None of it could be worse than the things he said himself. Certainly not when it came to his father.

There was something about this moment. This woman on this night.

Because there was something about *her* wanting to be done with this, even though he felt the same way. There was something about her wanting to be done with this terrible castle, with his family, too.

With him, was what he meant.

He didn't like how very much she wanted to be done with *him*.

But, "I can't wait to find out," he replied as he followed her to the window.

When she looked up at him, he had a sudden, spectacular vision of who she could be for him, if this was real. What kind of partner and ally she would be, if things were different. If they were what they seemed. What a glorious thing indeed it could be to be married to this woman.

But reality came in on the heels of that vision, hard.

Because Giaco couldn't have that, could he?

Because she wasn't wrong about him. He was made of lies. He couldn't be honest with her or anyone else. Not after so many years of waiting for this very moment.

That was not a possibility. And it meant that no matter how much he wanted her—and he was beginning to realize that wanting her had become the cornerstone of his existence—he couldn't really have her.

Because this game they were playing was one thing. But the woman he'd come to know while they played it would not accept anything less than honesty from a man who was her *real* partner. He didn't have to ask. He knew.

And all of this sat in him like lead. It was a sour taste in his mouth.

He hated it.

Giaco didn't think. He kissed her, taking her mouth with a kind of urgency he couldn't fully explain to himself, because he didn't wish to know himself quite that well. Not when there was so little he could do to change.

He kissed her instead, because she tasted like wonder. Like hope.

She tasted clean, like truth.

And more than that, she had somehow managed to insinuate herself so deeply beneath his skin that some days he thought that he had nothing at all in his mind but her.

Ivy was dressed as if she was a bride already, in exquisite cream from head to toe, and he couldn't bear it. He turned her around and sat her down on the window ledge, then knelt down at her feet. He looked up the length of her lush, lithe body to see all that wild heat in her blue eyes.

Giaco slid his hands up her legs, pulling up the hem of her skirt as he went. He stroked his fingers beneath the panties she wore, pulling them to one side to find that glistening heat that he knew waited for him there.

And then he leaned in and buried his head between her legs.

She made the most beautiful noise he'd ever heard. Her hips jolted, and then rocked against him as he licked his way deep inside her, and then ate his fill.

He lost track of the number of times she shook against him. The way her fingers dug in hard to grip his hair, leaving pricks of pain that he hoped he would feel later.

He lost track of the screams she stopped bothering to muffle, and he half hoped the whole castle heard.

If he could have broadcast to the world that everything between them was real, just like this, he would have.

When he finished, he tucked her swollen, sweet center away again, covering her with the scrap of lace he tugged back into place. He smoothed her skirt back down her legs and when he sat back to look up at her, she looked… disheveled.

It reminded him of that night in the study when she'd looked at him, all heat and desire. Like then, he'd thought she had never been more glorious. Except this time he could taste her in his mouth.

They studied each other for what felt like an eternity.

"Tell me," she said, in a voice that was little more than

a rasp after all that pleasure, while her blue gaze moved all over his face and made him feel as exposed as if she flayed him open, "why does this feel like a goodbye?"

Giaco made himself smile, though it sat on his face wrong. He could feel it. "I can't imagine," he said. This should have come easily to him. This was what he was good at. Blowing smoke. Flashing mirrors. "We marry in the morning. This is the very opposite of goodbye, Ivy."

But later, after he'd walked away and left her there—after he forced himself not to look back—he knew that they were both perfectly aware that he was lying.

Yet again.

CHAPTER EIGHT

LEONTINA WALKED INTO Ivy's rooms in the castle the following morning without an invitation, but with a cautious sort of smile on her face. "I hope I'm not intruding," she said, softly.

Ivy wasn't sure that she and her former stepsister and soon-to-be sister-in-law had ever had a proper heart-to-heart. Back in the day, growing up here, everyone had kept their head down and handled their own trauma. It wasn't much of a bonding experience. And this time around, though Ivy had spent a good deal less time in the castle, she'd only seen Leontina when Umberto demanded that there be so-called family gatherings. She still had the impression that the other woman deliberately kept herself to the shadows.

That she'd sought out Ivy of her own volition seemed like a significant shift. That alone would have intrigued Ivy.

But it was also Ivy's wedding day. And she very much wanted to stop thinking about the implications of that. The same way she didn't want to think about what had happened last night, either. Much less how it had ended, with Giaco walking away.

It had seemed prophetic.

"Of course you're not intruding," Ivy said, and waved

Leontina to a chair near hers in the sitting room that had always abutted the rooms considered hers here. As a girl, she'd never sat in here. It was too exposed. There was no lock on the door. She'd always preferred to hide away in her bedroom, behind a lock and beneath the covers of her bed—but that was a long time ago.

Today she was halfway through her preparations for a wedding that had felt real last night, with Giaco's clever mouth between her legs. Yet today, the profound fakeness of what they were doing seemed to weigh upon her like blocks of concrete hung from her shoulders.

She could have done without all these contradictory emotions altogether.

Perhaps that was why it took her longer than it should have to register that Leontina did not look the way she normally did. On the contrary. She was wearing a dress, and not the usual sort of dress she wore, shapeless and deliberately unforgettable. This dress was a bright magenta color that clung to her body, so that all a person looking at her could really see was her endlessly long legs in the high shoes she was wearing. It also called attention to her dramatically lithe figure that would not have looked out of place on a runway model or a prima ballerina.

It made Ivy wonder all over again if it was, in fact, genetics that gave Giaco his outrageously beautiful form. But she focused on the woman still standing in front of her, noticing the other major difference. Leontina did not have her hair scraped back into her usual severe bun. Today it was flowing all around her, thick, dark waves that fell halfway down her back.

"My God," Ivy said, a smile taking over her mouth.

"Look at you. You're absolutely stunning. I can't believe you hide all of this all the time."

Leontina smiled back, and that only drew attention to the dark jade eyes she shared with her brother. "Thank you," Leontina said in her quiet voice, though even that seemed to hit different today. It sounded far more intense, and measured, than Ivy remembered. "My brother doesn't get married every day. I thought I ought to represent the family right, though obviously, normally, I prefer not to be noticed." Color dusted her cheeks and she looked away down. "I also wanted to make you an offer. One that you can refuse, of course."

"What kind of offer?" Ivy asked, intrigued.

If her former stepsister, soon to be sister-in-law, offered her a getaway car, she honestly didn't know what she would do.

Instead, Leontina sat down on the chair Ivy had waved her to. She blew out a breath. Ivy tried not to feel self-conscious. Her hair was done and her makeup perfect, but she wore only a robe as Gabriele and the rest of the stylist battalion were doing something with her dress in the other room. She hadn't asked what.

She also hadn't imagined that she'd be entertaining anyone in this state, but she was too intrigued to let the small matter of being underdressed get to her.

"I wanted to offer my services as a stand-in family member," Leontina said, smiling at Ivy with what looked like determination more than anything else. "I know you don't have any. And I'm not entirely sure that you *like* Giaco all that much, which, fair enough. He's a lot. But this is your wedding. So if you feel like you wish you had family of your own, well, I did used to be your stepsister. And I always wished that things were different here. What I mean is, I can be family for you, if you like. If that would help."

Ivy had thought that it was a long shot that she would shed even a single tear at this wedding. Given that it was such a circus and had nothing to do with the two people getting married. And even if it had, said two people were putting on a show anyway.

But Leontina proved her wrong that easily, with her honest, earnest expression and the way she looked directly at Ivy. Ivy felt salt prickle the back of her eyes.

"I don't want to overstep," Leontina continued in the same quietly sincere manner. "But last night I found myself thinking that should I get married as my father insists I will, and at his command, what I'll miss the most is my mother. That made me wonder if you did, too. And she can't be here, I know. But I can."

The prickle behind Ivy's eyes became more of a threat. "That is the sweetest thing anyone could possibly have said to me today," she said. She reached out a hand to grab Leontina's, and it was like a new understanding bloomed between them. A new bond. She could feel it warm her, deep inside. Maybe this was what healing felt like. "*Thank you.*"

And after Leontina left, Ivy sat with that. The offer, the warmth. The notion that somehow, she and Leontina had become the friends they always should have been this morning. Even as Gabriele and his minions hurried her into her gown, and spent what she considered an unnecessary amount of time debating the fall of her excessively theatrical train, she kept coming back to that offer.

As if Leontina had figured out something that Ivy wasn't sure she'd known herself.

Or maybe she had, because she'd been telling herself all along that it didn't matter that she didn't have anyone at this wedding. It didn't matter because it wasn't a real wedding. It was just a game. A show.

A show she had to perform in, and beautifully, to finally have access to her money so she could pass it on to those in far greater need than she'd ever been.

So the fact that she had no father to walk her down an aisle and no mother to hug her fiercely and make her smile didn't matter, either.

She'd tried her best to believe it.

Because she could not quite accept that getting married to a man who she knew was only pretending to care about her—likely even when he touched her—made her feel some kind of orphaned all over again.

She told herself what mattered was what came when this particular circus show was finished. That was the only thing she should be thinking about.

But what she really felt as Gabriele ushered her down the steps of the castle, and outside toward the cleverly sophisticated altar that had been arranged in a beautiful spot overlooking the vineyards and the hills, was that she and Leontina had a lot of lost time to make up for. That really, that was something worth *feeling* about. And that when her sister-in-law got married—whether at Umberto's command or not—Ivy would be there.

Whether she was still playing charades with Giaco or not.

As she thought that, she saw Umberto sitting in the front row of the chairs that had been set up for this wedding, loudly holding court. And the enormity of what was happening here seemed to land on her with all its weight.

It was a charade, sure enough, but it was going to hurt.

Life in this castle had been every person for themselves. There had been no room for connection. Only survival. She had to assume that her marriage would be more of the same. Ivy already knew that when it ended, at the three-year mark she and Giaco had agreed to, her heart would be broken and she would have to find a way to live without the endless frustration and fascination that was Giaco.

She honestly didn't know how she was going to manage that. Not when she had barely slept last night, too aware of the tender place between her legs that he'd claimed so intensely, so completely.

And because she'd understood, as she'd watched him walk away, that this wedding was no new beginning. Not for them. What she didn't know was *how* he planned to leave her when they'd agreed to the same terms.

But when Gabriele hissed at her to look lively, Ivy headed down the aisle—on her own—and surrendered herself to one of the most over-the-top weddings and receptions she'd ever experienced in her life.

The only way to make it bearable was to remind herself that it really wasn't about her at all. Because it wasn't.

There were those moments when she and Giaco said their vows. There was that odd light in his dark eyes, and the way he looked at her when he slid a ring on her finger—but that was overshadowed by the spectacle that Umberto was putting on all around them.

Even Giaco seemed different, lost too firmly behind his mask today.

Ivy told herself that all she had to do was smile, look pretty, and pretend this was all happening to somebody else.

The reception was a whirl. Gabriele collected Ivy's train and bustled her dress so she could walk around, though she didn't see the point to it. She didn't know anyone here. She didn't care to know them. They weren't even the sorts of people that she would normally reach out to for donations to her charity. These were power-brokers on a different scale. They weren't here to talk about donations. They were trafficking in far higher stakes.

This meant that Ivy could excuse herself from having to do anything at all but observe.

She watched the vultures circle, particularly the women who clearly felt that they ought to have been Giaco's bride. Not content to simply throw dirty looks at her from across the bit of field near the vineyards that had been turned into a luxurious, tented reception area, they liked to come up and introduce themselves. So she could see their talons up close.

Ivy smiled and greeted each and every one of them as if they were long-lost friends. She wondered if this would hurt her more if she and Giaco actually had true feelings for each other. Or, at least, if they'd started that way. If it hadn't been an ice-cold business arrangement from the start.

Though as Ivy nursed her drink, because somehow she didn't think a fuzzy head would help with anything, she had to question her own characterization of the start of this whole marriage thing. Her memories of that day were not *ice cold* at all.

It was all Giaco naked. Then Giaco lounging on that

couch. And then the pictures that he'd taken, that she sometimes remembered as if they were the truth of what had really happened. As if the story they told was what had gone on between them when she knew it hadn't.

Or not then, anyway.

Her body clenched around the memory of his fingers. His mouth.

No, *ice cold* was not how she would describe this marriage at all. Nor was it all that *businesslike*—not according to any definition of that word she'd ever known.

This wedding, on the other hand, was both of those things.

After one too many rounds with the society women who went out of their way to let her know that they had sampled her husband—or wanted to, it was hard to tell the difference—Ivy retreated. She found a place to sit at one of the tables almost out of the tent entirely, where she could smile enigmatically the way her mother always had, looking both unapproachable and at her ease.

Truly, she thought, one of the greatest gifts her mother had ever given her. All the guests continued to look at her but they didn't come near her and for the first time since she'd woken up this morning, she felt like she could breathe.

She watched Umberto fawn all over a much younger man who looked to be about Giaco's age and who, unlike everyone else at the castle today, seemed completely unmoved by the Tavian influence. If anything, he looked stern and forbidding, as if he was the one taking the measure of Umberto.

This could only mean that he was the famous Pau Calixto, the morally upright Spaniard billionaire who was the reason Ivy was in a wedding dress today. Even more interesting, to her mind, was the fact that Giaco seemed to dislike him. He was busy charming everyone else at the party, but when it came to Pau Calixto, he looked… as if his famous magnetism was unavailable to him.

And here Ivy had always thought that Giaco could make it look as if he was intimate with anyone and everyone. No matter who they were.

When Giaco finally came to find his bride at her solitary table, he had done two full circuits of every last guest at this reception.

"You really do know how to work a crowd," Ivy murmured. "It's really quite impressive."

"I would have thought you'd be doing the same thing," he said as he came to stand beside her, then bonelessly slid into the chair next to hers.

The moment he was sitting, he was lounging. And he already looked rumpled, the way he always did. It was something she thought only outrageously beautiful men could get away with. Everyone else here was in formalwear, and they were adhering to all the rules of that kind of dress, but none of them shined bright the way Giaco did. If any of them had lost their tie or opened their collar or looked a bit as if they might have rolled around somewhere, they'd probably be so embarrassed that they would be going to the castle to change.

Giaco, by contrast, looked better than he had standing so properly at the altar. And he had looked pretty phenomenal up there, Ivy could admit. That was just a fact.

"This is not the crowd to hit up for donations to an orphans' charity," Ivy said with a shrug. "The women are feral and all want a taste of you. They are unlikely to support my endeavors. The men are too busy jostling for position around your father. They have no time to spare for the insignificant needs of the sorts of human beings I'm certain they find disposable."

"How astute," he replied in that low voice of his. "And you didn't even have to circle your way through the crowd to read them all so well."

She looked over at him, certain that she would see that mocking glint in his dark eyes, but felt a kind of shuddering inside her when there wasn't. He wasn't even looking back at her—he was looking down at her hand. Then he reached over and picked it up, playing with her finger that now sported two rings. That beautiful engagement ring he'd given her. And the platinum band beside it, its simplicity somehow as arresting as the stones.

He wore a platinum band on his finger, too. It was flatter and wider and equally absent any adornment.

Ivy hadn't felt much of anything up at that altar that the staff had made beautiful, beneath a pergola bright with summer flowers in bloom. It had all been rote recitation and a fervent wish that she did not have to do this while being stared at by so many people who quite actively wished her ill.

But this, here in a moment that was only theirs, felt hushed.

She felt something chime deep inside her, like there was a power in the rings themselves. As if there was a magic here she hadn't understood.

Ivy could have sworn he felt it, too.

But they were still at this reception. Being watched on all sides. She swallowed, hard. "You don't like your father's business partner," she said, to change the subject.

Giaco looked at her sharply, and she thought she saw something like surprise cross his face.

"Whatever do you mean?" he asked. "I make it a point of personal pride to have no awareness whatsoever of my father's business affairs."

"He's right over there," Ivy said, and she searched the crowd until she found Pau Calixto once more, standing in the corner talking to… Well. That looked like Leontina, though she was certain she was mistaken. She'd never seen Leontina talk to anyone. She pointed him out anyway. "There, by the fountain."

"Yes, yes," Giaco murmured, with only a quick glance that way. "I don't know him. I don't like his type. Prudish. Forever on the verge of a lecture. Deeply and surpassingly boring, at a guess."

She turned to look at him, because none of that sounded like him. He almost sounded as if he was parroting himself. Ivy shook her head. "That's a lie."

Those jade green eyes widened, and he looked at her in astonishment. Astonishment laced through with arrogance, that was. "You cannot believe that I would lower myself to *lie* about the tedious corporate shills my father surrounds himself with," Giaco said, sounding deeply offended.

"As far as I can tell," she retorted, "you will lie about anything. Everything. Is that not so?"

But the stare he leveled on her was interrupted when they were beckoned out onto the dance floor. Ordered, more like.

"I danced with your mother at her wedding to Umberto," he told her, almost abruptly. His eyes darkened when hers widened. "She was beautiful, of course, but also unnecessarily kind to a feral young man who wanted badly to hate her when it was, in fact, his father he loathed."

"My mother was always kind," Ivy managed to say, though there was a lump in her throat. She remembered the wedding too, though Umberto had thankfully ignored her. She smiled at Giaco. "Never unnecessarily."

More beckoning from the dance floor interrupted the moment. Ivy's heart was tripping in her chest and she had to wonder if, perhaps, that was best.

Because this wasn't in the itinerary, this memory of Alana. This wasn't part of the show.

In a show of obedience, Giaco rose. He led her out into the middle of the floor, took her hand, and drew her into his arms. And Ivy knew she ought to have been listening to the music or paying attention to the steps they were meant to be doing as they danced, but she didn't care about any of that. She was too busy studying his face.

His beautiful, impossible face.

"I don't understand how it is that you fool so many people," she told him, because it was that or weep over the gift of a story about her mother that she'd never heard before.

"I don't fool anyone," he replied, though she was holding on to him and she could feel the almost imperceptible way he stiffened. "What you see is what you get when it comes to me."

"That's not even a good line. It was obvious to me the moment I saw you again."

"Though perhaps not from the very first moment," he replied, his voice a silken bit of darkness.

Ivy wasn't immune to the way that curled around her.

How it sank deep into her and curled around and around until she was nothing but the heat he'd made.

But that wasn't the point.

"I actually wonder if that's why." She held his gaze. And even as he moved the two of them across the floor, with all of that elegant grace that seemed so effortless from such a powerful body, he looked very much as if he didn't see anything but her, either. "I saw all of you, and so it was impossible to see less."

"I hate to be indelicate on the day of our most blessed union," he said, his voice that dark blade that told her he was being deliberate. And likely provocative. "But seeing me naked is not exactly unique."

"I wonder," she replied. She tilted her head back and gazed at him. "You take such pride in showing yourself off but I'm beginning to think it's just a little bit of sleight of hand. If everyone is so busy looking at everything you show off and too busy concentrating on your antics, then they'll miss what you're really doing, won't they?"

She expected him to laugh at that, but there was something too sharp in his gaze. Then he twirled her around instead, which was no kind of reply. He twirled her out and then brought her in again, then dipped her low. And when he stood her up again, Ivy was dizzy and flushed and Giaco had that usual mocking curve in the corner of his mouth.

"What a fascinating line of interrogation that was," he said, as if he was devastated it had ended. "Alas, I do believe our duty calls."

There were more pictures, because of course there were more pictures. Elaborately staged affairs to make the most of the opulent elegance on display here. No doubt fodder for another puff piece that would make it seem as if Umberto Tavian himself had personally put together his own son's wedding ceremony and reception out of the goodness of his loving heart.

No one who had ever met the man could possibly believe he had a heart. But then, rich men did not have to be kind. They only had to stay rich and no one would care what they were or to whom.

Ivy couldn't wait to read about her own wedding in a glossy magazine, with pictures of herself that would look like a stranger.

Happily, soon enough, a helicopter landed out in the field and the staff loaded it up with bags they'd packed on their own with no input from Ivy about what she might need on a honeymoon. She was getting used to that now. Once the helicopter was packed, she and Giaco were helped on board. Where they could wave out at the crowd as they flew away.

It felt a lot like an escape.

The flight wasn't long and after what felt like a short while they were circling into a landing on one of the prettiest islands in the Tyrrhenian Sea and touching down on a landing pad where a sleek convertible with a stretching cat ornament on its hood waited for them.

This time, the driver was Giaco. Thanks to the itinerary, Ivy knew that Giaco had a small estate here on the island of Capri. When they got to his villa, Ivy was charmed despite herself. Most of it was windows, so that at every opportunity, its inhabitants could gaze at the sea. And more, down the hill at the village of Capri that clustered into the hillside.

Inside the main room, she turned her back on the view and stared at her husband. *Her husband*, something inside her whispered, as if that term had only now landed in her.

She folded her arms. "Do you know what I've been doing to pass the time today?"

His gaze seemed hot and dark at once. "I shudder to think."

"I've been counting up all the times I know you've lied to me, and it's quite a few. They keep coming and coming." Ivy considered him. "What I can't decide is if you're so busy wearing masks you can't tell the difference between a truth and a lie any longer. Or if you mean it. Every single lie you tell."

He stood there across the length of the room from her, and he didn't come any closer. "I don't know what you mean."

"I think that you do. And I think you might have miscalculated."

There was a flash of his smile. "Impossible. I never miscalculate."

"Everything we've done has been a group project," she pointed out. "Your house in Rome is filled with all of your people, all of the time. Your father's castle is even worse. We go on dates but we only pretend that they're private. We conduct ourselves in the glare of publicity at all times."

"That is because our affairs are publicity," he said, in that silken way of his.

"But now we are all alone. No staff. No intrusive family members. No paparazzi." She shook her head, almost as if she felt sorry for him. "You must be terrified. When your masks drop this time, you must know I'll see it."

To her shock, he didn't laugh. He didn't make one of

his typically off-color remarks. He didn't slink toward her, brandishing his sexuality like a club.

He stared at her, and she noticed his hands flexing at his sides.

"On the other hand," she said quietly, "I happen to know a bit about masks myself. I don't think that if you chose to go without yours here it would be the end of the world."

He moved toward her then, but without all of that grace of his. He looked…jerky. Uncoordinated.

Something kicked deep in her belly, but she didn't move. It didn't occur to her to move. He kept coming until he was standing right there before her, staring down at her.

"There is not one true thing stitched into me," he told her. "I am a patchwork tapestry of lies, so many that I cannot keep track. I could not untangle them all, even if I wanted to."

She could hear a loud noise and only belatedly real-ized it was her own heart in her chest. Pounding out a rhythm all its own. Slamming into her ribs. The closer he came, the louder it got.

"You don't have to untangle them all," she whispered. And this, then, felt the way she thought their vows should have. "Tell me one true thing, Giaco. Just one."

He moved even closer then, a look of such powerful intensity on his face that it made her heart stutter in her chest. Then he reached out and slid his hands over her cheeks, to hold her hair. To touch her.

"This," he said, sounding gruff and unlike himself. Or possibly more like himself, at last. "The only true thing I know is this. You."

And when he kissed her it felt like all the vows they'd made, writ large. It was as if she could *feel* them, now.

It was as if the kiss made them real.

He kissed her over and over and then he lifted her up in his arms and carried her through the sprawling, airy villa, stopping time and again to get his mouth on her. Until finally, everything spun around and they were both on a bed.

For a moment, they only stared at each other, and she knew that this was going to be different. That this time there would be no holding back. That everything had been building to this bright afternoon with the sun streaming in the windows and all that blue in the distance, but nothing but dark jade intensity here.

She felt her whole body shudder at that, while the heat of it all washed over her.

"You're my wife," he said, gritting out those words as if his life depended on them. "And you're wearing entirely too many clothes."

Wife, she thought. It sounded different when he said it like that. It sounded real, not like a charade at all.

It felt different when he pulled back, but only so he could pull her with him and stand her on her feet next to the bed. And she was absurdly grateful for every woman he'd ever touched, because it had taken a team to put her into this dress but Giaco had her out of it in a flash.

He stripped her down and stopped, gazing at the lingerie she'd put on in what seemed like a different life, back at the castle. It had been handed to her with the rest of the things she was meant to wear today and she tried to read the expression on his face as he stared at it.

"I assume you picked this out yourself," she managed

to say, though her voice sounded insubstantial. Breathy. "A groom's gift you already knew you would like."

He took his time dragging his gaze back to hers. "There is not one thing I don't like about pretty, flimsy silken things on a woman's body, but I was not expecting…this. You."

And then he showed her what he meant. First he shrugged out of his own clothes, and Ivy thought that having seen him naked before should have prepared her for the impact of it again, but it didn't. He took her breath away. Again.

Then again as once more, he knelt down before her and proceeded to worship her body as if he had never seen a woman before in his life.

There was no place his mouth didn't touch. No place his hands did not move, roaming all over her, making her glow with heat and longing.

When he slipped his fingers between her legs, he found her molten hot and wild. For him.

"Too pretty," he murmured. And then his fingers were thrusting inside her, making her breath hitch and her hips move to meet him, and it happened so fast. Giaco's fingers were a magic spell and her undoing at once, and she fell apart so quickly that it almost made her laugh. Maybe she was laughing. She couldn't quite tell.

Then he was pushing her back on the bed and crawling up the mattress with her until they were rolling all around. She wanted to put her mouth on him at last. She wanted him with a ferocity she couldn't explain.

Maybe it didn't need explaining. It was simply who they were, wrapped up in the heat of this. They were wearing nothing at all save the rings they'd exchanged and something about that made her feel…calamitous.

But the calamity felt like joy.

Ivy explored that chest of his, at last. She traced her way over all of those ridges and flat planes of muscle. She followed the sprinkling of dark hair all the way down to that giant cock that had been imprinted in her mind since she'd seen him come out of the water like something mythical.

And he was much bigger now.

But when she went to put him in her mouth, he stopped her.

"Not today," he told her.

"But I want—"

"Don't worry," he said gruffly. "We have a vast menu to work our way through. But today I thought we'd keep it strictly traditional."

A breath seemed to escape of its own volition. "Traditional," she repeated. "There's not one single thing about you that's traditional."

"It's the missionary position that's traditional, little saint," he said, as he moved up her body and settled himself between her thighs. "But not usually the way I do it. Yet I haven't been married before, either. It feels rather ceremonial, doesn't it?"

And she could feel the head of his cock as he worked himself into all of her soft heat. It felt so good, just like that, that she was shivering already. Her body was filled with sensation, so bright and hot she hardly knew what to do with it, and before she could say anything at all, he simply thrust deep inside her.

There was a shock of pain. A hot, deep tear.

Giaco froze. She froze, too.

There was nothing save the thunder of her heart and that overly taut feeling deep inside her. The sense of him there, filling her. Changing her. Her body forced to shift to accommodate him, and it did.

That thought made it better. She experimented, moving her hips, and that was better still.

"Ivy," he said, thickly. With a kind of sorrow. "Ivy, it never occurred to me—"

"Giaco," she whispered fiercely. "*Do* something."

So he did.

He started slow, a slick, deep slide. So slow that she was the one who got impatient as all of that heat grew inside her. She was the one who wrapped herself around him, crossing her ankles in the back and gripping him as tight as she could.

Until, eventually, he propped himself up on his hands so he could look down at her as he pistoned in and out of her body.

She loved it. She met every thrust. She lifted her hips to take more of him and it was like a wild flame, everywhere. Tightening. Tightening more.

Until, at last, he came down and gathered her close to him. Then he slid one hand between them and pressed down.

Hard.

And then there was nothing at all but stars. All of the cosmos, every constellation, and all of it somehow contained between them and in the two gold bands that marked them as married.

As husband, as wife.

As *one*, at last.

CHAPTER NINE

GIACO HARDLY KNEW HIMSELF.

They stayed in bed that first night. The villa had been stocked for their arrival and he knew that he could summon staff if he wished. But the idea of having people in the villa with them did not sit right with him.

Not when his most unexpected wife—his *wife*, a role he'd expected would be filled by some dullish sort of nun who he would have to work hard to pretend to fall in love with, but fate had given him Ivy instead—had shocked him with her innocence.

He felt…humbled. Altered in ways he was afraid to entirely examine.

Simultaneously unworthy to be in her presence, and yet certain that there was nowhere else he wished to go, nor would go.

A week into their honeymoon—that Giaco had decided to have in a place like Capri because it would lend itself to so many "accidental" photographs as they walked about the charming village and explored the island—they still hadn't left the house.

What they had done was explore—lazily, urgently— the menu that he had mentioned. They rose only to shower, or sit in the bath, or find their way out to the infinity pool, where it seemed as if they could float on the horizon forever as long as they were touching. As long as they were always, always touching.

They were insatiable.

Something about Ivy's wide-eyed wonder and heated delight made everything seem new to Giaco, too. Every time he touched her, it got harder and harder to recall if he'd ever touched another. He was creative, but she—

Well. She was a legend. And she was his wife.

In his experience, intensity depreciated at a rapid rate. Intensity required mystery, and once mysteries were solved, boredom set in. He had experienced this cycle more times than he—or anyone else—could count.

But there was nothing boring about Ivy.

Ten days into their honeymoon, they lay in their bed rumpled and panting. She shifted, then smiled down from where she lay stretched out on top of him. "There's a beautiful island out there," she said, pausing to kiss him. "I think we ought to explore it."

Giaco had the lowering thought that perhaps she was bored. That perhaps this wasn't about him at all.

He wasn't sure he knew what to do with that notion.

She smiled wickedly. "I want to see if we can take a walk like civilized people. Or if we really are the wild animals we seem to have turned into here."

And he laughed, because he laughed a great deal in her presence, it turned out. He wasn't sure he had ever laughed so much in all his life—not *real* laughter, anyway. It was one more reason why Ivy wasn't boring.

He tried, repeatedly, to demystify her. It never worked.

Giaco was fascinated by the way she *breathed*. The small noises she made while she slept. He was captivated by the difference in the way her collarbone tasted when compared with that sweet spot at her navel.

He could not seem to solve any of these mysteries. If anything, they only deepened the more time he spent with her.

So ten days in, they finally dressed. This took longer than it should have, because Giaco insisted on choosing her clothes and that led to him taking them off again, and so it was much later when they finally emerged from the villa and wandered their way down from the villa into the famous Piazzetta to take in the beating heart of Capri at last.

Giaco told himself that he needed to be on alert, making certain that they were seen. Reported upon. Made into myth and wonder for the consumption of the world.

But how could he remember something so tedious when Ivy walked with her arm around him, holding on to him as if she couldn't bear to let go? How could he concern himself with the grimy business of selling himself to the tabloids when every step they took felt so precious?

It took him another ten days to understand what was happening.

That she had worked some kind of magic on him, he could admit. That she had wrecked him when all along he'd been so certain he had the upper hand, he could grudgingly accept. That she had somehow turned him inside out and found her way beneath his skin when he least expected it—all of that he could come to terms with.

But there was only one word that really fit all the things he felt in her presence, and it was not a word he'd ever thought he'd have any sort of passing acquaintance with. Not about himself and his feelings.

Hell, Giaco had made it his life's work to pretend he'd never had a feeling at all.

He told himself that the reason this intensity did not fade away was simply because he knew it couldn't last. Because it wouldn't. It couldn't. She'd asked him if he was saying a kind of goodbye the night before their wedding and he had been, because he'd understood that their wedding was the start of a countdown that would end all of these games and schemes.

This was only a little bit of interstitial space as he waited for the phone call that would change everything. The phone call he'd been working toward his whole adult life.

This was a breath in between. It could never be anything else.

So perhaps it was unsurprising that it felt like more.

"You seem so pensive," Ivy said one night. They had ventured out again and if pictures of them had made it off the island, he wouldn't know, because he'd set his mobile to block every number save one. They sat at a restaurant that was right there on the pretty bay in the marina. They were both sun-kissed and bright, and he had spent the better part of an afternoon teaching her how to go down on him while he returned the favor on her.

This seems inefficient, she had complained.

It's an exercise in patience and restraint, he had replied.

An inefficient and tedious lesson, she'd retorted. *Did you know that you were this Catholic, Giaco?*

He had laughed, because she always made him laugh, and then made certain that she had better things to do with her mouth.

Now he reached over and took her hand across the small table, playing with the rings he'd put on her finger. It was an enduring shock to find how much he liked them there. The rings themselves and the very *idea* of this woman wearing his mark—this claim he'd put on her. He liked it more than he'd ever imagined he could like such a thing.

His mother had not raised him to think highly of the institution of marriage.

He had taken her around the island over these days that bled one into the next. They had explored the Roman ruins. They had driven through the rural splendor of Anacapri. They had climbed in the hills, lain out on the beaches, and found ways to have sex in a variety of public places like they were a pair of teenagers.

Though he couldn't recall having quite as much fun when he'd actually been one.

Normally, if someone accused him of something like *being pensive*, he would drawl something impertinent, change the subject, and have them wondering why they'd imagine him capable of such a thing.

But this was Ivy. "I don't feel pensive," he said. "Or not unduly so."

She leaned closer and propped her chin on her hand.

"Do you think it's Capri that has changed us?" she asked, with that directness and simplicity that killed him every time. "Or do you think we're not changed and this is simply a fun holiday, and when we go back we will simply…act as if this never happened?"

He found that his ribs hurt and he could not account for it. "I think that learning how to live in the moment, since it's the only thing we really have, is always wise," he told her.

Yet Ivy, rather than taking his sage counsel, rolled her eyes. "I love when you say things like that." Though her tone suggested that she did not, in fact, love it. "Because, of course, you like to make it seem as if you've lived only in the moment your whole life. But I know better."

"Ask anyone," he dared her, but not in his usual joking, careless tone. There was something else inside him tonight. It felt almost like a kind of grief. "I am reckless, untrustworthy, undependable, and impossible to pin down. I will run through your hands like water and leave no trace behind."

She shrugged. "That's not my experience."

He blinked, not sure if he was taken aback by what she'd said or that brisk tone she'd used. As if it was so obvious that she wasn't sure why she was even saying it out loud.

"I mean it," she said when all he could manage to do was stare at her. "You tried, back at the castle. You did your best, but that version of you that everyone seems to know is not at all believable once a person spends time with you." She tilted her head slightly to one side then and he had the strangest urge to pull his hand away from hers. That he didn't felt heroic. "But it seems as if *you* believe it."

And there were so many things he couldn't tell her. Secrets he had agreed to keep—secrets that had never been any hardship to keep. This had all been too long coming. It had taken years.

He wanted to tell her, but he didn't. He couldn't. It

wasn't that he didn't trust her—it was the simple truth that he didn't trust himself.

Giaco had kept his secret for so long that it had become a kind of superstition. He worried that if he shared it with anyone, for any reason, that would make certain that it all fell apart. That he would fail when he was so close to the end.

He didn't dare risk it.

He *couldn't* risk it.

But he also couldn't play his usual role with her any longer. Not after the weeks they'd spent on this island, wrapped up in each other. Not only would she not believe it, but for the first time in as long as he could recall, he *couldn't*. He didn't have it in him. Not now. Not when they'd learned so many truths about each other while they'd been here.

Everything on the island of Capri was bright. The sun, the sea. The colors of the buildings, the smiles of all the people.

The two of them were, too.

Sometimes he was certain that Ivy knew as well as he did that they could only stay safe if they kept away from the shadows.

"I know exactly who I am," he told her, and that was true. He played with her hand in his, moving her rings on her finger. "You asked me for no masks and I'm not wearing one. Maybe I am pensive, little saint. Maybe this is who I am when no one's looking."

"I'm looking," she whispered.

"But you are like the moon over the sea," he told her, not sure where the words were coming from—only that they needed to be said. That he *had* to say them, like they were coming from a part of him Giaco barely knew. "Not a spotlight or flashbulb. And don't you know? Everyone looks better in the moonlight."

She shook her head at him, and then leaned across the table to kiss him. It was sweet. It was perfect. It was only a kiss, and they were in public, so there could be no deepening it.

Not that the public part mattered as much as the *kind* of public this was. A restaurant was not a hiking trail. It was not a grotto off the beaten path where it was worth the risk.

That was not the sort of press Giaco wished to make.

So she kissed him, and they held hands over the table, and it was so simple. It was so *easy* to be here, sipping Capri spritzes beneath the stars while gentle music played. They ate food fresh from the sea and simple, perfect Caprese salads and talked of absolutely nothing at all—yet hung on each other's words.

And that was when Giaco knew.

Not in the storm of sex or the intensity of desire. Not that those things were absent in this moment. He knew they were never far.

But right now, in the sea air, it was as simple as the ringing of a bell tower calling out the hour.

It wasn't a feeling. It was a fact.

For the first time in his entire life, the most infamous despoiler of women in Europe was in love.

Head over heels, impossibly, and probably irreversibly in love.

That fact settled in him, and he let it.

When they finished their meal and headed back down

the ancient streets toward his car, he took her hand and guided her into the moonlight, away from the shadows.

They were there another week before the call came.

Another week of shadowless, impossible joy.

Then his mobile buzzed early one morning. Giaco almost pretended he didn't hear it—and that told him things he wasn't sure he wanted to know about himself. How much these weeks had changed him. How much *she* had changed him.

But the only way out was through. He had always known that. Really, that had been the point. Giaco had never anticipated meeting someone who would make him regret all these choices he'd made and committed to, long ago.

Or, if not regret them, understand that once he went through with this thing that he had been working toward for so long, it would change them, too. He could not see how it could not. For one thing, it would fundamentally disrupt the agreement that he and Ivy had made. He hadn't considered that a factor when he'd agreed to their marriage. He hadn't expected to *care*.

And little as he wanted to risk this now, he knew there was no choice.

He'd made this decision long ago.

It defined him.

Giaco rolled out of bed and he took his mobile outside, out onto one of the terraces that looked down at the sea that seemed to have become part of him now. Much like this island that didn't feel to him like a means to an end. Not any longer.

Nothing felt that way, and that was a problem, because the end was nigh.

He picked up the call and asked one question. "Is it ready?"

The voice on the other end of the call sounded as dark as Giaco felt. "It is."

Giaco rang off and stayed where he was, his hands braced on the rail before him.

He could see the hint of dawn, those bright summer colors streaking over the horizon, as if he was watching a painting in real time. Behind him, he knew that Ivy, his wife—*his wife*, and that mattered more than it should— was warm in their bed, that lush body of hers always willing, always ready, always somehow new.

But he had always known that this would end. He had always known that this day would come.

So he went back inside and he scribbled a note to her, then left it by the bed. When he was done he leaned over and smoothed her hair back from her face. She murmured something in her sleep, and then quieted when he kissed her on one flushed cheek.

Then he walked away, made a few terse phone calls to make arrangements, and drove away from the villa before the sun fully made it over the horizon.

Even when he was in the helicopter, flying high on his way back to the mainland, he was fully aware that he had left his heart behind.

Giaco would have sworn he didn't have one.

And now it didn't matter, because it was hers.

CHAPTER TEN

IVY DISCOVERED VERY quickly that Capri was not the magic.

Capri was lovely. Possibly one of the loveliest places she'd ever been, and she'd been lucky enough to see a great many spots on this planet that anyone with eyes would find stunning. But even so, it was just an island.

The magic, it turned out, was Giaco. And when he'd gone he'd taken it with him. All of it.

Leaving Ivy with…herself.

Her decidedly less magical self, who found that his absence meant she was suddenly called upon to figure out what, exactly, she planned to *do* with herself now that she was outside the tractor pull of this attraction she had to her husband.

When she'd spent most of her own life knowing precisely where she needed to go and what she needed to do.

It was a bit humbling to have spent no small part of her youth watching her mother lose herself in a man, and having assured herself that *she* would never allow herself to be at someone else's mercy like that. Only to discover that she was no stronger or better or more immune than anyone else. She had simply been lucky, before Giaco, never to encounter any man who could affect her like this.

Maybe it was more than simply a *bit* humbling, really.

His note had not exactly been illuminating.

An urgent matter to take care of, he'd written. *You know how to reach me.*

It was tempting to assume the worst. That he had lost interest overnight—something it seemed he'd done many times before, according to all available information about him. Ivy might have believed that she could read the intensity in him, that she could feel the way it matched her own—but he was *Giaco Tavian*.

Everyone who met him thought they knew him. What made her anything special?

Aside from the fact she was his wife, of course.

But the thing was, she knew that mattered to him. The way he always touched her rings. The way he called her *my wife* in that growly voice of his that never failed to make her heart skip a beat. If she stepped back from second-guessing herself because of his reputation and his past and thought about everything rationally, it made sense that he would simply take himself off to do whatever it was he did when he wasn't creating fantasies for the media to overdose on.

They had both agreed that this marriage would last three years, as required by the stern and upright Pau Calixto. It was what Umberto had promised the man and demanded of Ivy and Giaco. So whatever urgent matters Giaco had to attend to, the marriage would lurch along. Because it had to.

She assured herself that knowing such a thing was comforting. When the truth was, she did not feel the least bit comfortable, here in this magical place that felt more like exile without him.

It took her days to conclude that that *lurching* was all she really needed to focus on. The rules of their relationship had always been clearly outlined in the agreements they'd made with Umberto and, naturally, in the itinerary. What might or might not have happened on their honeymoon had no bearing on that.

Just because Ivy felt that they were in a completely different place now and would have sworn that he did too, that didn't change the fact that they were doing all of this for their own, very specific reasons.

That being a whole lot of money from a terrible, exploitative person they both despised.

She didn't think that finding herself alone on a gorgeous Italian island gave her the right to call Giaco up and demand that they change every aspect of the relationship they had both agreed on some time ago. Not just because it was her personal doom to be so deeply in love with him.

That wasn't the sort of magic that left when he did. It felt a lot more like a curse, and it had not exactly improved during their time on the island. Quite the opposite.

Ivy hadn't had the slightest idea that it was possible to love another person like this.

Heart. Mind. Soul.

And every last centimeter of her body.

A not inconsiderable part of her wanted to rage at him for doing this to her. For making her laugh. For teaching her all the things two bodies could do together, an ever-changing adventure through emotion and excitement. For making her understand that she was the best version of herself when he was a part of her, and how was she supposed to pretend she didn't know that now?

How was she supposed to pretend she was still the same person who'd seen him rise up out of that hot pool like a Roman god returned to earth to rule at will? She couldn't. Ivy wanted to share her feelings about that with him, too.

But he would have to come back for her to rage at him about anything.

And he didn't.

Finally, a week after she'd woken up to find him gone, Ivy decided that she was done with this. She felt a similar surge of clarity to what she'd felt the night of her mother's funeral, when she'd looked around at the guests in the castle—and the family that had never been hers in any real sense—and had realized that the only thing that tethered her to these people was gone. She didn't need to stay and suffer with them.

She didn't need to do anything with any of them, ever again.

Five years ago, that had felt like freedom. She tried to tell herself that this did, too. Because the more she thought about it, the more she thought that she never should have demeaned herself like this. She never should have put herself in a position where Umberto could direct any part of her life.

Yes, she wanted her inheritance—for good reasons—but she wasn't sure that it was worth all *this*.

Because even if she could accept that she'd made a practical decision for all the right reasons, she certainly never should have fallen in love with the biggest man-whore of all time.

That was the part that was inexcusable.

The thing she really should have remembered, all throughout their time on Capri, was that Giaco was particularly talented in playing a role. *Of course* she thought he was falling in love the way she was. What was the man but a mirror? He showed everyone he encountered exactly what they wanted to see.

Once she accepted that unpleasant truth, clarity was simple.

And something like urgent.

She left the villa, taking nothing with her but a change of clothes, and didn't contact any of Umberto's or Giaco's people. Why bother, when she didn't intend to involve herself with Umberto or Giaco after this. She walked to the Piazzetta, a long and pretty amble down from the villa, and then took the funicular down to the bright and colorful marina. Once there, she got herself a coffee in her favorite café and considered her options.

She'd known all along that Giaco was like a drug and yet she'd imbibed freely. He'd been slightly more than the oversexed clown he played for the tabloids, just slightly more human, and she'd dropped her guard completely.

As if she hadn't grown up in that castle, subject to his little reigns of terror every time he'd come home and turned things inside out. Simply because he could.

"You're a mess," she muttered to herself.

How had she managed to forget that she hated that man?

She boarded the first ferry she could, but she had no plans to go on to Rome once she made it to Naples. Instead, Ivy did the exact same thing that she'd done five years ago. She figured if it cured her once, it would again. She bought herself a ticket in the airport and flew home.

Not the home that she'd been so sure, secretly, that she and Giaco were building together. But the one she'd made for herself, to save herself, once before.

Ivy landed at Heathrow on a grim, rainy sort of summer day and told herself it was a great comfort after the glare of all that Mediterranean sunshine. She slogged her way onto the Tube, and only remembered when she walked from the Tube station nearest to her road that there might very well be paparazzi hanging around when she got to her house. But when she drew closer, she allowed herself a deep breath because she didn't see anything that would suggest that.

After all, it had been a while. Paparazzi were no doubt off somewhere, eating out of Giaco's hand. If she really fancied it, she could look him up online and see where he was, what he was doing, and who he was doing it with—

Yet surely that was a recipe for misery.

Because even though she knew how he choreographed his appearances, she also knew how convincing his act was. Why would she want to see it?

"Why do you *want* to see it?" she snapped at herself, and realized then that she was lurking on her road, talking to herself, and would likely scare the neighbors into calling the paparazzi themselves.

She let herself into her house and then stood there, leaning with her back against the door. It was quiet and dim inside and she told herself that she could breathe at last, but when her lungs didn't seem to respond to that the way she thought they should, she decided she was simply exhausted. Ugly tired, even. She went upstairs, wrinkling her nose because her house didn't smell right anymore. It didn't smell like *hers*. It smelled musty and shut up and very much like it belonged to a stranger.

Ivy decided that, too, had something to do with how deeply exhausted she was. She ran a bath, had a soak, and then put herself to bed.

But she dreamed of Giaco and woke restless and yearning time and time again throughout the night.

In the morning it wasn't bucketing it down outside, but it was still gray. She rummaged about for some kind of breakfast in her kitchen, but Giaco's people had cleared everything out when they'd swept her off all those months ago. She had to make do with a bit of instant coffee and some dry crackers.

Rather a comedown from the magically stocked villa, she had to admit.

She walked to the charity's offices, picking up a proper coffee on the way, and decided that it perked her up considerably even if it wasn't quite the same as the *caffè shakerato* she'd become enamored with on Capri. Ivy felt much better almost at once, and told herself that in no time she would have her life back and running the way she liked it. Thoughts of Giaco would fade over time, or until she was presented with a new itinerary, and they would manage their marriage that way until they were done.

Ivy was caffeinated and *looking forward* to throwing herself into work so she could hasten this process along.

But once she arrived at the charity, she found that everything was running swimmingly without her. Exactly as she'd planned all along, having gone out of her way to hire the very best people to do this work that she continued to feel was so important.

The last time she'd needed to escape the Tavian family, she'd created the charity. It had taken all of her time and attention.

It hadn't really occurred to her that she wouldn't have that option this go-round.

"Did you really come here without that delicious husband of yours?" asked one of her directors, smiling wide. "We were sure we'd get an inside peak at all that marital bliss since we know you."

"I'm afraid not," Ivy had to respond, with a little laugh and a big smile, neither of which she felt. *There you go*, a voice inside whispered. *Apparently you're just as much a liar as he is.* "He couldn't accompany me this time."

And after planning to go and make herself useful for the whole day, she found herself leaving again after an hour and finding herself roaming around Central London, as damp and gloomy as the weather.

She really did hate him, Ivy decided. He wasn't even here—she had no idea where he was, as a matter of fact—and yet he'd still managed to ruin her safe space for her. It was unforgivable.

Ivy spent another restless night in Kensington, but even though the sun came out that following morning, she couldn't settle. She felt…inside out. More than that, it was like she was *marked*. She'd gone ahead and married the man and now she was linked with him. No one who knew her in London wouldn't also know of her change in circumstances because the entire world knew about her wedding, and she didn't think she could bear discussing it.

Because he could be anywhere. Doing anything. They had both promised Umberto discretion. Not abstinence.

And she hated herself for thinking that. If she hadn't gone ahead and foolishly fallen in love with him, what would she care what he was doing?

Yet the reality was that she cared entirely too much, and that was why she booked herself on the Eurostar and headed for France. She took the train under the Channel into Paris and the fast train down to Nice with glorious views as they approached the Côte d'Azur.

Once there, she didn't go to Cap Ferrat. She found herself a room in an old hotel in Nice the way her parents had one year, according to the stories her mother had told her. She tried to recreate those memories of hers that were not true memories of what happened, but memories of the tales Alana had shared with her. Of the nights she and her mother would cuddle in Alana's bed and Alana would talk of markets in the streets, of macarons in colorful lines in glass bakery cases, of echoey hillside villages, of lavender fields, and the gleaming coastal walk from Nice to Villefranche-sur Mer.

Ivy was looking for her mother on the breeze or out there in the sunshine that dappled the blue waves, but she didn't find her. Not the way she wanted to. Not the way she had before.

Still she let herself wander, avoiding any hint of tabloid gossip or snarky papers. It was just her and the sea. Her and her memories. And as she sat on a bench near the water, in a place no one alive knew to look for her, she found something else instead.

Her poor heart.

Her optimistic, foolish heart that had hated Giaco

Tavian for all the right reasons—and would love it if she could hate him again.

But she didn't hate him.

She couldn't hate him—and she'd tried.

When she understood that, she understood her own mother, too.

Baffling as Ivy had found it, Alana really had loved Umberto. Her memories told her that truth whether she wanted to face it or not. Maybe not as time went on, but at first, the man had made Alana feel safe. He'd vowed to cherish her, and had not revealed until much later that the way he cherished anything was to collect it and forget it. But long before that became clear, Umberto was the first man since Ivy's father who had made Alana seem…peaceful.

That was a realization Ivy didn't want any part of, but she couldn't escape it once it came to her. Once the inescapable truth of it settled into her bones and stayed there. She found herself staring out at sea where sailboats danced on the waves and the larger, overwrought yachts of the very rich slid by like planets orbiting the sun.

Umberto had made Alana feel safe, and even happy, for a time. Maybe they'd had a chemistry that was inexplicable to anyone on the outside—the kind of chemistry Ivy could never have understood until now. But what Ivy knew for a fact about her mother was that Alana had never been mercenary. Alana had loved deeply or not at all. She had put her heart into everything she did and it had made her weak in a way, Ivy supposed. It had been her greatest strength and her greatest vulnerability. It had made her the luminous actress that she was and it was why her legend would continue long after Ivy was forgotten.

It was also the legacy that Alana had left her daughter.

The ability to love against all odds, in the face of adversity—and in many ways, Ivy thought, without hope.

There was nothing weak about that, Ivy understood now. It was a wild and terrible strength. And it was no wonder it was hard for Ivy to accept what was happening to her now, because she'd shut her own heart off on the day she'd watched them put her mother in the ground.

Looking back, she couldn't even have said what specific thing had happened at the funeral to set her off. All she'd known that day was that she was done. She couldn't stay in the place where her mother had died, married to a man who had treated the woman who loved him so much, against all reason, like an afterthought at best.

But the way that Umberto had behaved had nothing to do with the way Alana had loved.

Ivy understood that more in this moment than she ever had before. More than she would have been capable of understanding a few months ago. Maybe she'd needed all of this to happen with Giaco so that she could finally see her mother as she'd really, truly been.

Flawed, certainly. Insecure and needy, also true.

But when Alana Amis had loved, she had loved with every single part of herself and she'd never given up. Not ever.

Not even if it was patently obvious that the man she loved was not worthy of her.

Standing there in the South of France where her mother had told her once that she'd been conceived in the deepest love imaginable, Ivy stopped thinking about what she *should* do. What she *ought* to do. What would be the *strong and powerful* thing to do, as some kind of response to Giaco's departure.

Instead of all of that, she listened to her poor, broken, wildly optimistic heart instead, because it still believed in magic.

She still believed in magic.

And then she went back home. To Rome.

Because she could love Giaco enough for both of them. She had her mother's heart, and lucky for her, she was more resilient than her mother had been.

And it was high time to prove it.

CHAPTER ELEVEN

GIACO HAD WAITED his whole life to walk into a conference room in a gleaming corporate office set high in a skyscraper—this one in the Area de Negocios de la Castellana in Madrid—and finally turn the tables on his father.

He and Pau Calixto had planned this since they'd met at university. They had lived on the same stair at Cambridge and had met because they were both predisposed to taking long walks in the middle of the night. By the time Giaco was inevitably sent down in disgrace, he and Pau had cemented a lifelong friendship.

His friend, no stranger to the issues of legacies and difficult fathers, had suggested a remedy years ago. The catch was, it would take a long time. It would require that Giaco show the world the worst parts of himself—his basest urges and lowest moments—and claim they were the sum total of who he was, so that Umberto would never think to suspect his son *capable* of plotting against him.

The shameful truth about that was that he hadn't minded being seen as the most disreputable man alive. Not at first.

But then again, a man never fully understood the contours of his prison cell until the door was locked tight behind him.

Today, his friend gathered up a few items from his desk and nodded toward Giaco, who stood by the window with Madrid far below his feet.

"Are you ready?" Pau asked, in his usual ruthless, formidable way.

"I've been ready since bloody university," Giaco replied.

Pau only nodded at this. It had been a long road, but they were at the end of it. All that was left was the big reveal that would turn Umberto's world upside down and keep it there. *The good part*, Giaco always said, *will be the look on his face.*

"Five minutes," his friend told him. "We will start with some niceties to make certain he is not prepared. This will hurt him more once all is revealed."

There was nothing else to say at this point. They had plotted this out, every moment of it, across years. Their plotting and planning put Giaco's dating-to-wedding itinerary to shame. Nothing had been left to chance. They had set a trap for Umberto and lured him in, and now all that remained was telling the man that what he thought was a win on his end was, in fact, a severed limb.

They'd distracted him with Pau's supposed purity tests and the clamor and commotion of Giaco's very public romantic life while they'd pulled the rug straight out from under Umberto's feet. They had always planned on a wedding that would seem like a surrender on Giaco's end, but the fact that Umberto had managed to manipulate Ivy Amis into it? Fate had clearly been on their side.

This day, this revenge, was nothing but sweet. Giaco had anticipated he would savor it forever.

His friend walked by and slapped him on the back, then nodded toward his wedding ring. The one he was forever fiddling with, and not because it bothered him the way he'd assumed it would.

"Will you tell her the whole truth?" Pau asked. "The whole of the game? Umberto will almost certainly hold on to her inheritance out of spite."

Giaco frowned. He hadn't exactly *forgotten* Ivy's virtuous reasons for marrying him, but he'd set them aside. He had been working toward this day for so long that he'd developed a kind of tunnel vision. Nothing that didn't serve the end goal mattered.

The fact of the matter was, Ivy was the only thing he'd seen outside that tunnel in years.

"Let's handle one problem at a time," he said, and put his hand on Pau's shoulder for a moment. They looked at each other, a whole lifetime of working to get *right here* between them.

Pau nodded again, and then strode from the office to get it all started.

And for the next five minutes Giaco stood quietly in his friend's office, looking out at the city below him once again. But this time without seeing it.

Because strangely enough, none of this felt the way he'd expected that it would. He had dreamed about that call he'd received in Capri for long years before it had finally happened. That everything was in place. That it was done—all done and dusted, save the gloating. He had fantasized endlessly about the joy he would feel once he knew that triumph was right here, right within his grasp.

He'd been pretty focused on the gloating, too.

But instead, it all felt...hollow.

He twisted the wedding ring on his finger. Surely all he needed was this confrontation with his father. Once that happened, it would feel the way it should.

That was the missing piece, he was sure.

At the appointed time, he walked directly to the conference room and let himself in, sauntering into the middle of a scrum of dark suits, all bespoke and understated.

Giaco, naturally, was in battered jeans.

For a moment, everyone inside the room fell silent at the sight of him. The *fact* of him, no doubt. What, after all, could Umberto's feckless tabloid-fodder son have to do with the serious business men like this trafficked in daily?

Giaco looked around, taking in the looks of incomprehension on so many dark-suited faces. He saw the gleam in his friend's gaze. Then, at last, taking his time so he could best savor what was to come and hold it close forevermore, he turned his attention to his father.

Umberto stared at him, his cold eyes without comprehension. "Have you gotten lost on the way to a whorehouse?" he asked starkly.

"Not exactly," Giaco murmured. He stood there a moment, making sure everyone was looking at him. Reliving his greatest tabloid scandals, no doubt. Only when he felt they were all sifting through his greatest hits did he take his time ambling around the table to take a seat next to Pau.

He let the awkwardness and confusion build as he lounged there, smiling faintly.

Pau waited even longer.

"I think that it is time I introduce you to my partner," Pau said, eventually, with his usual quiet menace. When Umberto barked out a laugh, Pau's dark eyes gleamed even more. "Giaco brings many things to this particular deal, I think you'll agree."

"Has he notified the paparazzi that he actually entered a building in which business is done?" Umberto asked, acidly. "I was unaware this fool possessed any other skills."

Pau gazed at the man who had been a nemesis to the both of them for too long to count. He did not smile, but Giaco knew him well enough to sense his deep pleasure. "Not only is Giaco a full partner in my business, *Signore* Tavian, but he's a majority shareholder in yours."

That sat there, in the center of the conference table, like so much lead.

"Some fathers teach their sons how to be men," Giaco murmured into the tense silence. "Good ones, even, or so I am told." He smiled at his father. "What you taught me was how to play shell games with money and, better yet, how to hide my true nature in plain sight."

And he could see it then. He could see the dawning awareness on his father's face that he had been outplayed. The contracts he'd signed when he'd come into this room repeatedly over the past week, filled with his usual gloating arrogance, had in fact signed away a significant portion of his fortune. If not most of it. The rest of it was tied up in real estate, but this partnership had been meant to ease Umberto's latter years. Then carry on his name forever.

Giaco watched his father play all the usual chess

games in his head and then come up with the only pos-sible answer.

"This is revenge," he gritted out. "But you would have had to set this up…"

"A very long time ago," Giaco agreed. He leaned for-ward, and made sure that his father was staring straight at him. He took a moment to enjoy the way that vein bulged on his father's forehead. It felt like a blessing. "I didn't like you very much to begin with, but after my mother died?" He shook his head. "I don't believe I have ever hated anyone more."

"Your mother was mentally ill." Umberto bit that out.

"I believe that," Giaco retorted. "Insofar as I believe that spending that much time with you would cause men-tal illness in anyone. As far as I'm concerned you might as well have shot her yourself."

And then he settled back to enjoy the shouting—and the vast joy he expected would accompany it.

But that, too, didn't land the way he'd imagined it would. It took Giaco longer than he cared to admit to re-alize that where he'd expected to feel a fierce and over-arching joy, he felt nothing.

Except empty.

Much later, after the magnitude of what Giaco and Pau had pulled off had been made abundantly clear to Umberto—rendering him little more than an old man frothing at the mouth, impotent and deeply aware of that fact—the two old friends were back in Pau's office. Pau poured them both the stiff drink they deserved and they clinked their tumblers together.

"And now you can be anyone," Pau said. "No longer

must you play the dissolute reincarnation of Pan, wreaking carnal havoc wherever you go."

"The world is mine," Giaco agreed.

Yet as he sat there, his own words came back to him. Words he'd said flippantly to a scrum of reporters within sight of the Spanish Steps. Words he'd used to paint a picture, to build a narrative.

Empty words, he would have said if anyone had asked.

But now, as he sat in Madrid with his best and only friend, having finally achieved what he'd expected to be the crowning achievement of his life, he realized that every word he'd said that day was true.

I never expected to fall in love, he had told a pack of mercenaries, in service to the story. Always the story. *But now that I have, I naturally wish to be with her. Always. I want forever, immediately.*

He had not slept much since leaving Capri. Ivy disrupted his dreams. He woke with her taste in his mouth and her scent in his nose and found himself alone in a hotel bed.

It was like leaving her all over again, every time.

But as he'd told those reporters months ago, instant gratification had always taken too long as far as Giaco was concerned.

He had never felt that so keenly as he did now.

"I must go," he told his friend abruptly. Then he left Pau staring after him as he stood up and left the office. He had already called for his plane before he got on the elevator. The flight was interminable, and his people were waiting on the ground.

It was not until he was being driven back into the Eternal City that it occurred to him to wonder if she would even be there. He had left her, after all. Given her no instruction or invitations to do anything. For all he knew she could be…anywhere.

The notion did not sit well with him.

He stormed into his house and glared at Gabriele, who always endeavored to meet him when he returned. And Gabriele, who was well used to Giaco's moods, stared right back.

"Where is my wife?" Giaco demanded.

"She's here, of course," Gabriele said, with exaggerated and rather pointed calmness. "She got back yesterday."

"Got back from where? Capri?" Something in him turned over uncomfortably at the thought of her on that island. *Their* island, as far as he was concerned, but by herself.

He didn't like that, either.

"My understanding is that she was in London and then sojourned a while in France," Gabriele said lazily. Then he lifted a brow. "But you will have to ask her yourself."

Giaco laughed, and clapped his assistant on the shoulder. "I believe I'll do that. Why don't you take the week off. Or the rest of the month."

"Is that a possibility?" Gabriele asked dryly. "Will your antics permit me to take a holiday of even the next quarter of an hour?"

"I suppose we'll find out," Giaco tossed back at him.

He started to walk past his assistant, but Gabriele stopped him. "Incidentally," the other man said, "the housekeeper wanted me to inform you that Saint Ivy has moved all of her things into your room. Herself."

The two men gazed at each other, and Giaco reminded

himself that Pau was not his only friend. Gabriele was, too. And the approval in his friend's gaze meant more to him than he could express—particularly as Gabriele's blessing on anything at all was hard to come by.

But clearly his best and most trusted assistant—and friend—was delighted at Ivy's return, too. And Ivy herself, it seemed.

It wasn't that Giaco *needed* approval, but the truth was, he had lived a long time with only its opposite. Tonight he took it in and let it seem to fill him up, like a tuning fork deep inside.

He didn't say another word. He inclined his head at his friend, then he simply turned and headed for his bedroom.

For Ivy, at last.

He bounded up the stairs and took the long hallway that led to the suite of rooms that sprawled over the back of the house. The suite that he'd had built for himself, never imagining that he would share that space with anyone. Now he couldn't think of anything he'd like more.

There were already fantasies drip-feeding into his head. Ivy waking up with him every morning. Ivy coming out of the shower. Ivy reading her books and taking her calls and leaving that scent of hers everywhere. Always.

He was so hard it hurt.

He charged into the suite and threw open the bedroom door, and there she was.

At last, *there she was*.

That joy he'd been chasing flooded him then, vast and hot.

Ivy sat up quickly when he threw open that door, her

blond hair cascading all around her and drawing his attention to the silken chemise she liked to sleep in—a detail that had plagued him this last two weeks—and then they were staring at each other.

He looked deep into all of that impossible blue, and now he had something to compare it to. The beautiful blue waters off Capri, turquoise and green, and still her eyes were more beautiful.

There was no contest.

"Ivy—" he began.

"I figured it all out," she said quickly. Ivy moved in the bed, kneeling up as if she wanted to run to him but didn't dare. He couldn't quite process that. "I don't think that Capri has to be a dream we had. I don't think things have to change."

"They absolutely have to change," he thundered at her. "You have no idea—"

"Here's the thing," she said in that same urgent way, and she sounded something like frantic. "I can love you enough for both of us. I don't need you to love me back. I can love you however you need to be loved. Wherever you go, whatever you do. I'm not saying it won't hurt, but I'll love you anyway, Giaco."

He stared back at her, something like awed and humbled at once.

And also furious.

She pulled in a breath. "I've been thinking about it, and I don't think I would have agreed to this arrangement if it was anyone else but you. Don't you see? I'm already used to loving you even when it makes no sense."

"Who taught you this?" he asked, not sure he could speak until the words came out of his mouth.

She shook her head. "I don't know what you mean."

"I have no desire to be loved like that," he said—except it sounded as if he was shouting. Maybe he was. He wasn't sure he cared. He wasn't *acting* with her and that felt a lot like jumping off a very tall building. But he didn't want to stop. "I don't want someone to love me *even though* it hurts them. I don't want to be loved *despite* the fact I'm apparently so broken that I could betray the person I've made promises to without a second thought. I don't want to be loved *because* I am broken."

She frowned at him. "I don't understand. I think it could be beautiful."

He moved toward her then, coming so that he was on the bed too and leaning over her, his fists on either side of her folded legs. Directly in her lovely face.

"I want to be loved fiercely and possessively," he growled out at her. "I want to be loved with expectations. Of fidelity. Of trust. Of intimacy and honesty. I want to be loved so much that a single lifetime cannot contain it and anyone who happens to venture near it cannot help but bask in it, too. I want to be loved so hard that my own children admire it. That's the kind of love I want, Ivy. And I warn you, I won't settle for anything less."

"But…" She shook her head, and he could see that there were tears in her eyes. They made his heart hurt. "I can love you as best I can, but—"

"I want that love, Ivy," he said, leaning in close to cut her off, "because that is how I love you. That is how I will continue to love you for the rest of our lives. I just spent over a decade convincing the world that I'm useless so that I could take revenge on a man who could not, for the life of him, love my mother enough to make her want to live." He moved closer still. "I don't want any part of that kind of love. I want *you*. I want *us*. I want everything we had in Capri, every day, always."

He reached out with one hand and touched her, and everything was immediately better with her cheek in his hand. The heat of her seeping into his skin. "I don't want any half-assed, sacrificial martyr shit, my little saint. The only crosses I ever want to see you climb on in this marriage will be for fun, not self-flagellation. Do you understand me?"

"Giaco..." she whispered, and the tears were flowing from her eyes then. He could feel them on his hand. "You took revenge? This was all *revenge*?"

"You have never been anything to me but light," he told her urgently. "Even in the midst of darkness. I swear it."

"I don't think you understand," she replied, and then changed the whole world again with a smile. "Am I to assume that it worked?"

He took in her smile and found his own mouth curving in response. "It was a triumph in every regard."

"And here I thought I could not possibly love you more," she whispered, her eyes damp. Lest he forget that Umberto had not loved Ivy's mother, either. That they shared this very specific burden. That she, too, had every reason to celebrate this win.

It made him feel a whole lot more like celebrating than he had before.

"All you have to do is trust me," he promised her now, in a low voice. "That's it, and I acknowledge that most would laugh at the idea. But I swear to you, Ivy—I swear that I will do everything in my power to be worthy of that trust."

She blew out a breath. He thought he saw her shiver. Then she was moving closer herself, and putting her hands on him, too.

"I love you more fiercely than you could possibly imagine and I have no intention of letting go," she told him, with notes of that ferocity in her voice. He could feel it in him, too. More of that joy, and far better because none of it was tainted with the years of revenge. This was all his. And she wasn't finished. "I want our children to be happier than we ever were, Giaco. I want to raise them to know, always, that joy is an option worth fighting for. But most of all, I just want you."

"You're in luck," he told her, allowing his smile to take him over, and all of it was real. Because this was real, and true, and theirs. "You already have me. We're already married. And the only thing we have left to do is make sure that everything that comes after is steeped in joy."

That was exactly what they did, tucked up in his bed, with the future all around them like moonlight, making them glow on into forever.

CHAPTER TWELVE

IVY NEVER KNEW how Giaco convinced Umberto to release her inheritance, only that he managed it. And it only took a year or two.

She gifted most of it to her original charity in London. And with the rest, she sought out other charities that she could bolster, too.

"Not because I'm a saint," she told her husband when he teased her. "Because I'm not. Definitely not." Given what they had just done to each other in the marital bed, there was no denying that was true. "But I see this as dispensing my mother's love as far as it can go."

"She would love that," Giaco said, and kissed her.

Ivy knew she would. She could feel Alana's love inside her, bright like a guiding light.

It took longer than the originally agreed-upon three years for the world to begin to accept not only that they were going to stay married, but that Giaco Tavian really had calmed down. That he really had taken himself off the market, turned a new leaf, and become not just a better man but the perfect husband.

There was much mourning across the land, gnashing and wailing, but there were far more people who watched the two of them and saw something beautiful.

"All it takes is the right person," he liked to tell the paparazzi, who clearly missed his exploits. "Then it is easy to find great beauty in the life you lead without having to attempt to amuse yourself with quantity rather than quality."

Ivy laughed when she read that quote in the paper.

"You really do love to torture all of your acolytes," she said. "You know they conduct grieving rituals on a daily basis, praying for my downfall."

"If their prayers worked, I would have found them more interesting in the first place," he replied.

And then demonstrated what he meant by *great beauty* right there on the floor of their library in Rome.

Ivy never returned to Umberto's castle. She didn't miss it, either. She certainly didn't miss *him*. Though she did take Leontina up on her offer to be the family she was missing. It turned out that the relationship they should have had when they were girls was easy now that they were grown women.

Suggesting that it had been all the external forces in that castle that kept them apart back then.

It was five years after their wedding, on her thirtieth birthday, when Ivy discovered that she was pregnant. And Giaco loved a celebration. He threw her a birthday party, then whisked her off to the villa in Capri, the place they still thought of as *theirs*.

And so she told him there, where the fact that they were in love had been impossible to deny any longer, that they were going to be a family all their own.

He grinned at her, holding her against him in that dreamy pool and running his hands down her sleek, naked back.

"Fantastic," he said. "I can't wait to taste you when you're ripe."

It turned out that he quite liked that taste. So much so that she spent most of her thirties having his babies. Four wild boys who looked just like their father and two little girls who also looked like their father, though some of them had her blue eyes.

They also adopted some of the orphans who stole Ivy's heart, to the point that some of their detractors in the papers made snide comments about their *home for wayward youths*.

But they wouldn't have it any other way.

Having been raised in that cold, isolating castle, no amount of family was too much. And love never ran out, like a tap. It only grew and grew.

Their life was loud. Hectic. But any time they began to feel too far away from each other, they found each other again. In their bed at night. And in that villa on Capri. They loved each other wildly, brightly, ferociously.

Time did not dim it. Age only made it glow.

They always held hands. They very rarely went to bed angry. They spent precious few nights apart.

And over the years, Ivy found herself profoundly grateful for her mother's legacy. For a heart so big that it could hold all of the people that Ivy was lucky enough to love. But she couldn't think of that legacy without a pang of sorrow, too. Because she knew that her mother had not always had the love that she'd given returned to her as she deserved.

Not the way Ivy did. Fierce and hot and deeper every day, because forever wasn't nearly long enough for Giaco and his little saint to love each other as much as they wanted. As much as they needed.

Though they gave it their very best shot.

* * * * *

Did you fall in love with To Have & To Hate*?*
Then you're sure to enjoy these other
sensational stories by Caitlin Crews!

Kidnapped for His Revenge
Her Accidental Spanish Heir
Forbidden Greek Mistress
An Heir for Christmas
Sicilian Devil's Prisoner

Available now!

*Keep reading for an excerpt from
Caitlin Crews's most recent title,*
King's Heir of Hate*!*

CHAPTER ONE

HIS MAJESTY XAVIER TADEO SANTIAGO did not have to make it all the way up the drive to the remote manor house in the farthest reaches of the royal estate to know that it was far past time to divorce his queen.

The drive itself was a pageant of early spring flowers flung in all directions like a discordant quilt. They were clumped here and festooned there, their bright colors clashing with each other and running all over the place, making a dramatic visual cacophony on both sides of the drive.

He found them offensive at once.

Tadeo was well acquainted with the work of the groundskeeper and his staff. They kept the rest of the royal estate in pristine and orderly condition, as was right and proper, since the royal family served its subjects and was called to present—always—their best foot forward. These grounds belonged to the kingdom. As did the palace, its contents, and indeed, the royal family itself.

Even the king himself was no more or less than the property of the kingdom, or so Tadeo's father had always taught him.

It meant more with the ghost of Tadeo's mother hanging always between them. The spectacle she'd made of herself. The shame and scandal she'd rained down upon the palace and the kingdom. His father had done his best to remain stalwart in the face of her behavior—always an uphill battle.

Now it was Tadeo's duty to take up the mantle that his father had carried until the day of his death five months ago. It had taken him all of this time to feel comfortable in the role that he had been preparing for all his life. It had required all of his focus and commitment to make the transition from his father's reign to his own as seamless as possible. There had been the somber funeral, then the burial, then the typical period of mourning.

But spring was coming. The Kingdom of Bellaza was coming alive after its cold, hard winter.

Tadeo needed to divorce his wife and move on—though, to minimize scandal and disruption, the divorce would have to be civilized. He had already plotted out the messaging with his team, and he had come to do this unpleasant task in person because he felt that was appropriate and a husband owed a wife that much. He assumed that it would be an uncomfortable conversation, perhaps, but a brief one.

After all, he had made it perfectly clear during their widely publicized courtship that this was precisely what would happen once he became king. They would play the part of a royal couple so well-suited to each other that their subjects made up happy endings for them—though there would be precious few public displays as they went about their official duties. Tadeo's family was well known for its adherence to the strictest protocol. They would let the public make whatever meal it liked from perfectly polite and expected touches.

Tadeo had been told there was fan fiction about their private life all over the internet. He chose not to know what that was.

But this marriage would end. They would never see each other again once they navigated their way through a divorce so amicable it would be applauded. He'd already spent time with his team plotting out the details. Once the divorce was handled, after a suitable period of reflection, Tadeo would find a far more suitable queen and set about making the heir the kingdom required.

He had spent seven years making certain that he saw Esme only when required to for the work they did, never in any private capacity that could lead to complications in his plan in the form of the child he adamantly did not want with her.

Well, a voice in him chided, *you managed it for* almost *all of those seven years, anyway.*

Tadeo did not wish to think about that one slip, five months ago. There were other, more pressing things at the moment, like the fact that the condition of the manor's grounds appalled him. More than that, the sight seemed to dig beneath his skin, as if she—and he knew it was her, if not with her own hands, then at her express direction—had planted all of the flowers in as unorthodox a fashion as possible *specifically* to bother him.

Queen Esme, betrothed to him since the day of her birth, his wife for the past seven years—and for one reckless year across an ocean in a foreign city, his lover—was astoundingly good at bothering him. She had a talent for getting under his skin in a way no one else could. Or ever had.

A reality that he had never come to terms with, though

he had learned how to control his reactions to her over the years of their marriage. Tadeo, in truth, did not wish to come to terms with the ways Esme got to him. None of that mattered now.

"It all ends today," he assured himself, his voice a dark spool of sound in the interior of the car.

He was glad he was alone.

Tadeo had driven himself, waving off his usual guards because he did not intend to leave the royal estate. Now, still on the garish drive, he slowed the vintage Rolls-Royce that had been a part of his grandfather's collection and ordered himself to find his center. To remain calm.

Something that was normally not the least bit difficult for him.

Only Esme disrupted his equanimity. Only Esme forced him to confront the distasteful evidence that he truly was his mother's son, made of all the wild, impossible parts of her that had led her to make such a display of herself for all the world to see. He loathed that he possessed such depths inside himself and had spent most of his adult life doing all that he could to keep them locked away.

He could not be the king his country deserved unless and until he removed Esme from his life. He had known this going in, but there had always been so much investment in the fairy-tale notion of the Prince of Bellaza marrying the Princess of Clarebonne from the neighboring kingdom. Not least because the two kingdoms had been one, long ago, and this only added to the fairy-tale mystique. After the scandal his mother had wrought on her marriage and therefore also on Tadeo's father's reign, a fairy tale had seemed like a gift. A gift that could fix what his mother had broken.

But the fairy tale had run its course. Now was the time to act, and Tadeo was ready. He was more than ready.

Their marriage would end quietly. There were no children after seven years of living completely separate lives in private, so there was no claim to the throne to worry about. Esme could go off to make a mess of whatever she wished, wherever she wished to do it, without it having any bearing on him.

Just so long as she left Bellaza and Tadeo never laid eyes on her again, he would be happy.

Because he would finally be able to *breathe.*

He would not let her damned flowers get to him, reminding him of too many things he did not wish to think about. All of them involving Esme and that recklessness only she conjured up in him. He would see to it that her gardening additions were summarily removed as soon as she left the manor house and replaced with a tidy hedge. There would be no sign of Esme's disruptive presence once she left, and that was what mattered. This chapter of his life was finally ending.

And not a moment too soon.

The drive wound around at last to the house itself, which was a fine old Bellazan structure made in the late medieval period, then renovated time and again in the centuries since to suit the whims of a succession of queens. When Tadeo had handed it off to his brand-new queen on their wedding night, it had been a sturdy, quietly elegant monument of the kingdom's history. He had not been here since.

An oversight, clearly.

Tadeo was not certain that he could entirely believe his own eyes as he gazed out at the monstrosity that loomed before him at the top of the drive.

She had…painted it, if that was what it could be called. What she'd done was gaudy. It was an *assault*.

In place of the expected white walls and red-tiled roof-tops that nodded toward the kingdom's Spanish neighbors, plus the hint of the nearby French countryside in the sprawling gardens that would not look out of place surrounding a chateau, the Queen's Manor House—once considered the refined jewel of the royal estate—now appeared to have been vomited upon by an intoxicated rainbow.

Tadeo was so aghast at the tasteless horror show in front of him that he almost forgot to step on the brake in the car. He rolled to a stop only centimeters from crashing into the insufferably bright magenta wall before him. He continued to stare out through the windshield, not able to accept that he was truly seeing the ornate, excessive, and expansive palate of too many colors before him.

He wondered if it was possible that he was, in fact, having a stroke.

At least that sensation was familiar.

It was much the way he had felt the morning after his father's death five months ago, when he had woken to find that it wasn't a dream. Not only was his noble and admirable father truly dead, when the old man had always seemed so invincible, but Tadeo had actually gone and done the one thing he'd vowed he would never, ever do.

He had allowed Esme into his bed. Or rather, a couch in his father's study, but it was the same regret either way.

Tadeo knew better.

God help him, did he know better.

He could recall that morning perfectly. How he had lain there on the couch in the study where she'd found him after the funeral, feeling as if he was fracturing into a thousand shards of jagged glass as she curled up at his side. She was so peaceful. She looked like an angel as she slept, the way she always had.

She still fit against his body perfectly.

It seemed impossible, after all those years, and yet there was no denying it.

Tadeo had felt as if his chest was cracked wide open, and she was to blame for it.

Just as she had been the first time, years ago, when they'd finally met each other on the other side of the world. He had been doing his graduate work in the sort of business, economics, and public policy issues that could only serve the kingdom. She had been an undergraduate in the same city. A city that seemed like a long-lost daydream to him now. The Boston of his memories was always covered in towers of snow to mark its bitter winters. There were no mountains to speak of, when Bellaza was ringed with them. More, the wild Atlantic was forever seething about at the end of streets and in the distance, as if keeping watch.

He liked to tell himself that he had been happy to leave that strange, small city—but he still woke up from dreams that smelled like the salt marshes of Cape Cod on a quiet spring morning, or sounded like the rattle of the T, or had him remembering walking along the Charles River on a picture-perfect fall afternoon.

Tadeo exited the car outside the manor house, shutting the driver's door sharply behind him. Then realized that he was standing about because he wasn't used to arriving anywhere and not being immediately greeted by staff. He was quite certain that there was staff at the manor house. What he did not understand was why none of them made themselves known as protocol demanded.

Thoughts of Boston felt like a reprimand, but then, he had known at the time that those years were an indulgence. That he was permitted to indulge in a kind of freedom there—the independence to walk where he pleased and live a life with far less scrutiny in a country not his own. He had known he never would again.

Still, he found himself shaking off unwanted memories yet again as he started for the main door, painted in a revolting shade of pink. If he was a vindictive man, he might have been tempted to make Esme pay to restore the house to its traditional state before releasing her. But that would only prolong this.

And to Tadeo's way of thinking, their entire relationship had already been entirely too prolonged.

He had known that he was betrothed since he was a child. He was five years older than Esme and had been shown pictures of her over time. She had been raised in Clarebonne, which was even smaller than Bellaza and had always enjoyed favorable relations with it, dating all the way back to the time in antiquity when the kingdoms had been joined. Their betrothal had been speculated about in the press all throughout their teenage years because it was not a formal, legal betrothal in the old style. It was an understanding.

An understanding between two kings was as good as law, in some places, but the two kings in question had been very deliberate about the way they'd handled Esme and Tadeo. The two of them had not met. They were deliberately kept apart, in fact.

No one expects you and Esme to molder on shelves, at least until you meet, Tadeo's father, King Hugo, had always said. *You can enjoy yourself as you wish, as long as you remain* ever-conscious *of your duties and* scrupulous *about your reputation.*

Yes, sir, Tadeo had murmured. He had been all of fourteen and did not wish to think about his duties any more than necessary, given he had already found them crushing. Much less his spotless reputation, though that part he was admittedly more concerned with.

King Alain and I are agreed that you and Princess Esme should meet when she is finished with her studies. What that means, his father had said, perhaps more sternly than before, *is that you may do what you wish, but you should never be linked in public with another woman. Neither one of you must ever be seen in any kind of amorous situation, or in any questionable position that could be interpreted the wrong way. You might find this onerous. But it is excellent practice for your future.* His craggy face, with the blue eyes Tadeo had inherited, had been somber. *I expect there to be no scandals, Tadeo. Not one, not ever. Do you understand?*

Tadeo had always understood.

He had only been eleven when his mother had died, off in a boating accident in Italy with one of her many lovers. Some had claimed that Tadeo was too young to understand what was happening then, but they were mistaken. He had understood completely. And even if he hadn't, he certainly would have heard every sordid detail at school, where his status as crown prince had long since lost its luster.

Even if he'd wished to avoid his mother's exploits, he'd been unable to.

For years at that point, it had been impossible for Tadeo to avoid the sordid details that his mother seemed to have no shame sharing with the whole world. Everybody knew the story of the selfish, unsatisfied Queen of Bellaza who had provided the kingdom with its needed heir and then declared her duties and responsibilities completed.

The rest of my life is mine, cries the Queen! the headlines screamed.

Tadeo had understood completely and totally that he could not, as that queen's son, create that kind of scandal. No matter what.

Even if he hadn't been told exactly that by his father, repeatedly, he would have come to the same conclusion himself. The kingdom prized its calmness. Its peace. Scandals were for other, more volatile nations.

It was Tadeo's duty not to become a scandal. He took that seriously.

He had therefore enjoyed himself, but always with women who understood his position. And who, more to the point, he trusted not to sell him out to the papers. This meant that he was significantly less of a player than many of his boarding school friends, but he would not be the one to put the family's name into the mud again.

He had vowed it after his mother's funeral. It was the first, last, and only time he had ever seen his father cry. Or, more precisely, allow his eyes to look damp. For the smallest moment.

Tadeo had learned over time that there were warning signs when a woman he might have been interested in was the wrong choice. Bright red flags that would indicate when a woman was appropriate for him or not, and it was his duty to look for those flags and react accordingly. He liked the women he dated, very privately, to be circumspect in all things. Modest, practical, and smart enough to think twice when it came to exposing him.

He had never chosen wrong.

If it had been up to him, he would never have chosen Princess Esme.

Tadeo had been the one to initiate their meeting in Boston. He'd been in graduate school across the river in Cambridge and even though he did not go out of his way to keep up with the Princess's every move, he could not avoid knowing that she was attending nearby Wellesley College, a very highly selective women's college with an august reputation.

His palace handlers—now his team—made certain he knew.

They were both far away from the intense press interest that surrounded them in their own countries. They were both still immersed in their studies, so there would be no chance of accelerating the march toward their wedding. Tadeo had thought it would be safe. Easy. A smart move to build a friendship in advance, so that the years they would spend together as husband and wife could only be better for it.

Too well had he understood the point of the stories King Hugo had told about his own courtship of Tadeo's mother. Lady Marisol had not been his family's first choice. She had not been a choice at all. She had been impetuous, bright, and bold. The King had fallen hard and had insisted that he would marry her or he would not marry at all.

But soon enough, Marisol had grown bored of royal life. Just as everyone had warned the King she would.

What had followed had haunted his father for the rest of his life, and now haunted Tadeo too. The ghost of Marisol was what lay beneath every decision and every plan Tadeo made for his life and his reign. He thought about the scenes she had made, the extramarital affairs she had flaunted, the contempt with which she had treated the kingdom in general and his father in particular, and vowed to do whatever was necessary to protect the kingdom from a repeat of such embarrassment.

He had married Esme because their kingdoms were invested in their wedding, a choice he would make again if necessary. Just as he would divorce her now because she could never be an appropriate mother to his heir. She was too difficult. Too…problematic.

Back in Boston, Tadeo had possessed absolutely no desire to repeat history. He'd had no intention of ever allowing the kind of passion that had blindsided his father and made him turn his back on his kingdom for the pleasures of the flesh to level him as well.

He had been completely and totally unprepared for Esme, in other words.

Another familiar feeling he very much wished to banish from his life entirely.

No servants appeared at the door, or responded when he knocked, so he opened it himself and went inside. And in case he'd imagined that the exterior of the building was the only place that his wife had allowed her creativity free reign, he was quickly disabused of that notion.

The color scheme—though that word, *scheme*, suggested some kind of a plan, which Tadeo doubted very much had been used here—continued inside. He walked through, finding that his jaw was tense and that he was grinding his teeth as he looked from one ruined room to the next. There was nothing in the whole of the historic house that she had not changed.

Nothing.

It felt like a metaphor for the way she had laid waste to Tadeo's own principles and self-regard.

Tadeo hated fucking metaphors.

Though as he walked through one atrium that bled into the next, with more floral theatrics at every turn, he knew that he could not lay that solely at her feet. The woman could be as wicked as she liked, but it was the wickedness in him that had met hers.

He was the one at fault. He accepted that.

Now he wished to be done with it. There was no doubt a sweet, unassuming, deeply boring heiress somewhere that he could marry and never think about again. She would do her job and leave him to his. They would have a pleasant, comfortable, smooth sort of life, marked by nothing but the milestones of their children and the peaceful prosperity of the kingdom.

He could almost taste it. All that was needed was the quietly amicable divorce he had planned, with tasteful statements to the press about going their separate ways with no acrimony and the best of wishes for the other's happiness, etcetera, and he could have peace at last.

At last.

On the other side of the ruined house, he stepped outside onto one of the back terraces and surveyed the gardens as they stretched out toward the horizon and the Pyrenees in the distance.

It did not take a degree in landscape architecture to realize that the gardens, too, had been changed.

In seven years, Esme had completely transformed the sophisticated, manicured gardens that previous queens who had lived here—excluding his mother, of course, who had never set foot on this property while the gleaming shores of the Côte d'Azur existed—had enjoyed. They had all taken pride in overseeing the tending of these gardens, always passing the torch along to keep them quiet, contemplative. A fitting place of respite for a queen. A place for meditation and relaxation.

There was nothing the least bit *relaxing* about the gardens greeting him now.

They were a deafening bugle of early spring exuberance.

There were daffodils and crocuses and cherry blossoms, and they were everywhere, bright and bold. Unseemly and overwhelming, Tadeo thought darkly, and he could not understand why he could not find a single, solitary soul to explain to him what was happening here.

He knew that Esme had not gone on a trip of any kind. Her schedule went through his office, for his review. The palace had only just begun taking on their outward-facing duties again as mourning for the late King had only this week come to an official end.

Esme should have been here. Doing whatever it was she did with her time.

Which was, he reflected now, wrecking heritage sites

with the wanton application of tawdry colors slapped about with no thought whatsoever for the lines of the garden or its pathways or its internal logic, apparently.

He stood still in the not precisely warm air of the late February morning, generating more than enough heat on his own. The sun was already warm, hinting at the fairer months to come. The chill of winter almost felt like a memory when the sunlight moved over his face.

Tadeo needed her excised from this house, and the kingdom, and his life before another season passed. If he allowed himself the sort of dramatics he felt only when he was in Esme's vicinity, he would be tempted to think his own life depended on it.

"But I do not allow it," he growled out at himself. As a reminder he should not have needed, yet clearly did. Another reason this long, torturous chapter of his life needed to end.

He thought he heard a sound in the distance and he made himself walk toward it, scowling at the once-orderly flower beds everywhere, now showing no restraint or any evidence of planning. It was all too bright. Too out of control. As if someone had spun around in a circle like a child with bubbles, flinging seeds about.

The image he had then, of Esme doing exactly that, did not help his mood any.

Tadeo battled his way down an overgrown pathway where vines had been encouraged to do as they liked, making his way out toward the far end of the gardens, where a pergola sat between the garden proper and the start of the vineyards that some enterprising queen had insisted be grown here some while back. They did not produce a lot of wine, but every year, the queen's vintners produced a specialized run of limited-edition bottles of the queen's Pinot Noir. It had long been seen as something of a status symbol among certain sets in the kingdom's society.

Tadeo half expected to find the vines torn up and discarded in favor of an amusement park or something equally hideous, but they were still there. Waiting for the summer to ripen into grapes suitable for wine.

He heard voices again and strode toward them, feeling more and more like a storm cloud as he went.

Then he walked up through the vine-laden path to the pergola and found his wife at last.

She was sitting at the long table in the shade there with what appeared to be her own staff members. There was food and drink on platters, but there were also swathes of fabric, and Esme herself seemed to be wearing half of them.

It took him long, heart-pounding moments to realize that he was reacting to two things at once. One, he had no idea what they were doing, and no one seemed to look at his direction or even notice he was there, which was unusual. Two, and more concerning, it was impossible not to notice that Esme looked...well.

Very well.

Glowing, in fact.

And his body, his temple that he preferred to keep completely under his control at all times like a bit of marble that he alone could sculpt, betrayed him yet again.

The way it had from the start where Esme was concerned.

Because every time he laid eyes on this woman, it was like he was burned alive. She was a poison in his blood, a curse upon his soul, and a great lamentation in the cock that he otherwise ruthlessly controlled. If *a great lamentation* was what to call it when he was nothing at all but hard and needy while the woman was doing nothing but sitting in a chair across a table from where he was standing, with very little of her visible aside from her face.

Damn her.

He waited. Esme didn't look up. She was talking animatedly to one of the women dressed in black beside her. They were both moving their fingers over the fabric that was swaddled all over as if they'd been draping it over Esme on purpose, but he couldn't hear what they were saying.

It was possible he had stood there a long while before a different woman altogether looked up, met Tadeo's gaze, and gasped.

"Your Majesty!" she cried.

He watched the ripple effect as it happened. First everyone froze. Then, as if lit by the same flame, all of the servants leaped to their feet—pushing back their chairs so there were loud scraping noises against the tile patio, then dropping into deep, deep curtsies.

His queen, Tadeo noticed—his *wife*, though hopefully not for much longer—did not rise, though it was protocol that she do so. Esme stayed where she was, draped in so many different shades of billowing fabric that he could barely see her body beneath it.

"Leave us," Tadeo told the staff, and did not watch them as they all fluttered off, like so many dark-feathered birds. He kept watching Esme. He studied her maddeningly perfect oval of a face with her dark flashing eyes and that lush, impossible mouth that he absolutely could not feel all over his body, because that was insupportable.

"Have you taken up sewing?" he asked her, not convinced he was entirely in control of his voice. He blamed her for that, too.

The proverbial straw on a camel's back.

"I'm redecorating a room," she replied.

In that same serene voice of hers. Brimming with that same abominable confidence that he found both atrocious and wildly compelling.

Tragically, she also remained the most beautiful woman he'd ever encountered.

This had been true when she was but a sophomore at Wellesley. It was even more true now. It was an outrage on every level, but she still looked like the model of the perfect woman, should he have been asked to draw such a creature.

Should *drawing* be one of his talents.

It was not that she was the most beautiful woman in the world, he supposed. But it was a cruel trick of fate that she managed to hit every single one of the buttons Tadeo had not entirely realized he had until he'd met her. She was elegant. She was graceful in everything, from her smallest gestures to the way she laughed—a sound that came from her belly and transformed her whole face. She had the sort of exquisite manners that were necessary for the circles they moved in, but Esme always made them seem as if they were innate.

As it was not something she was *doing*, but something that was simply a part of *who she was*.

She had been kind to his father, who had been less enticed by the *fairy-tale* argument and had been largely chilly in return. She was always kind to their subjects, no matter what sort of questions they tried to ask her while she was shaking hands and playing her part. It was his cross to bear that she also looked equally as stunning when she was in jeans and flats as she did in a bespoke gown made for ceremony and circumstance.

Today, she had her dark, glossy hair piled casually on the back of her head. It looked like she was wearing a simple T-shirt, which seemed to hug her curves more than usual. And yet she still simply emanated sophistication from every pore.

Only Tadeo knew that there were ways to touch this woman that lit her on fire. Only he knew what she looked like, her dark eyes glazed over with sex and longing, her mouth open while sounds of desire poured out, and how she writhed beneath him, taking more and more until he wasn't certain if either one of them would actually survive—

But that was not the point of this visit.

"My father has been dead for five months," he told her curtly.

"Five months and thirteen days," Esme replied. Oddly specific, to his mind, but she said it so calmly. Her lips curved. "I am aware, Tadeo."

If he could go back in time, he would not have given her access to his family name. By the end, only his father still called him that in person. Most of his friends from school called him variations on his title. Or other nicknames of one sort or another.

The press, of course, used all of his names as they pleased.

He could have had her call him by his proper first

name and he often thought that would be easier, because he wouldn't feel this tug of undeserved familiarity. Maybe the name alone would have done it. Maybe then he would never have become familiar with her at all.

But he couldn't go back to that first dinner in a quiet restaurant overlooking the Charles and fix what happened.

He could only do the necessary damage control now.

"I told you long ago that we would remain married only as long as necessary," he told her, no longer caring how dark he sounded. It needed to be done. It didn't matter *how* it was done. "I've come here to let you know that I intend to begin our divorce proceedings. Immediately."

Tadeo didn't know what he expected. For her to cheer, perhaps? Sometimes he convinced himself that she was no more interested in continuing this marriage of theirs than he was. Perhaps he thought she might cry? After all, he hadn't been so far gone that he'd forgotten the things she'd whispered in the night after his father's death.

Sometimes he thought those words haunted him.

But of all the possible responses he'd imagined, it wasn't the way she smiled at him.

Her lips curved gently. Even kindly, he thought.

And then she rose.

The fabric cascaded off her and slid in heaps of shimmering color to either side of her, landing on the tiles at her feet.

But Tadeo forgot all about that. He couldn't take his eyes off her.

Because the Esme he had last seen five months ago had been lean and lithe and in some way resembled the ballet dancer she had once told him she would have liked to have become, in a different life.

She stood, the fabric fell, and she placed her hand on the shelf of the belly—*her belly*—that had swelled up to enormous size. A great deal as if she had a ball beneath her shirt, when, of course, she did not.

It was impossible. It was inconceivable.

It was a disaster of epic proportions and she was *smiling*—

"About that divorce," Esme said, as if they were discussing the weather. Or what to have the staff prepare for a snack. As if she was not very obviously *pregnant*. "I wonder if you might want to rethink."

Get up to 4 Free Books!

We'll send you 2 free books from each series you try PLUS a free Mystery Gift.

FREE Value Over **$25**

Both the **Harlequin Presents** and **Harlequin Medical Romance** series feature exciting stories of passion and drama.

YES! Please send me 2 FREE novels from Harlequin Presents or Harlequin Medical Romance and my FREE gift (gift is worth about $10 retail). After receiving them, if I don't wish to receive any more books, I can return the shipping statement marked "cancel." If I don't cancel, I will receive 6 brand-new larger-print novels every month and be billed just $7.19 each in the U.S., or $7.99 each in Canada, or 4 brand-new Harlequin Medical Romance Larger-Print books every month and be billed just $7.19 each in the U.S. or $7.99 each in Canada, a savings of 20% off the cover price. It's quite a bargain! Shipping and handling is just 50¢ per book in the U.S. and $1.25 per book in Canada.* I understand that accepting the 2 free books and gift places me under no obligation to buy anything. I can always return a shipment and cancel at any time. The free books and gift are mine to keep no matter what I decide.

Choose one:
☐ **Harlequin Presents Larger-Print** (176/376 BPA G36Y)
☐ **Harlequin Medical Romance** (171/371 BPA G36Y)
☐ **Or Try Both!** (176/376 & 171/371 BPA G36Z)

Name (please print)

Address   Apt. #

City   State/Province   Zip/Postal Code

Email: Please check this box ☐ if you would like to receive newsletters and promotional emails from Harlequin Enterprises ULC and its affiliates. You can unsubscribe anytime.

> ## Mail to the Harlequin Reader Service:
> **IN U.S.A.:** P.O. Box 1341, Buffalo, NY 14240-8531
> **IN CANADA:** P.O. Box 603, Fort Erie, Ontario L2A 5X3

Want to explore our other series or interested in ebooks? Visit www.ReaderService.com or call 1-800-873-8635.

HPHM25